Dear Reader,

Twenty years!

Despite appearances to the contrary, Joan Hohl and Kasey Michaels are not joined at the hip. However, we are very good friends and bosom buddies, and have been for more years than either one of us cares to remember. And so, imagine our delight when we received the call about doing interconnecting stories for the twentieth-year celebration of the Silhouette Romance line.

Over the years, we have spent many, many hours on the telephone, talking about our separate writing projects, bouncing ideas off each other and generally brainstorming. But always for our individual projects, never for a collaborative effort, although this has always been one of our dreams.

And the dream, as it became reality, was just as much fun as we'd always thought it would be. Laughing, joking, making up characters in our heads. Giving them life, giving them problems…and most of all, giving them their happy endings.

We sincerely hope you enjoy our creations as much as we enjoyed creating them. It has been work, it has been frustrating at times—but it has been a lot of fun, too. And surprisingly enough, at the end of the day (and at the end of our stories) we are still very good friends and bosom buddies.

Best,

Kasey Michaels   *Joan Hohl*

Dear Reader,

Our yearlong twentieth anniversary celebration continues with a spectacular lineup, starting with *Carried Away*, Silhouette Romance's first-ever two-in-one collection, featuring *New York Times* bestselling author Kasey Michaels and RITA Award-winning author Joan Hohl. In this engaging volume, mother and daughter fall for father and son!

Veteran author Tracy Sinclair provides sparks and spice as an aunt, wanting only to guarantee her nephew his privileged birthright, agrees to wed *An Eligible Stranger.* ROYALLY WED resumes with *A Royal Marriage* by rising star Cara Colter. Prince Damon Montague's heart was once as cold as his marriage bed…until his convenient bride made him wish for—and want—so much more.…

To protect his ward, a gentleman guardian decides his only recourse is to make her *His Wild Young Bride.* Don't miss this dramatic VIRGIN BRIDES story from Donna Clayton. When the gavel strikes in Myrna Mackenzie's delightful miniseries THE WEDDING AUCTION, a prim schoolteacher suddenly finds herself *At the Billionaire's Bidding.* And meet the last of THE BLACKWELL BROTHERS as Sharon De Vita's cross-line series with Special Edition concludes in Romance with *The Marriage Badge.*

Next month, look for *Mercenary's Woman*, an original title from Diana Palmer that reprises her SOLDIERS OF FORTUNE miniseries. And in coming months, look for Dixie Browning and new miniseries from many of your favorite authors. It's an exciting year for Silhouette Books, and we invite you to join the celebration!

Happy reading,

Mary-Theresa Hussey

Mary-Theresa Hussey
Senior Editor

Kasey Michaels

Joan Hohl

CARRIED AWAY

Silhouette

ROMANCE™

Published by Silhouette Books
America's Publisher of Contemporary Romance

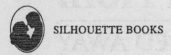 **SILHOUETTE BOOKS**

ISBN 0-373-19438-2

CARRIED AWAY

"Logan Assents"
Copyright © 2000 by Kathryn Seidick

"Ryan Objects"
Copyright © 2000 by Joan Hohl

Visit Silhouette at www.eHarlequin.com

Printed in U.S.A.

CONTENTS

"Logan Assents"
Kasey Michaels

Books by Kasey Michaels

Silhouette Romance

Maggie's Miscellany #331
Compliments of the Groom #542
Popcorn and Kisses #572
To Marry at Christmas #616
His Chariot Awaits #701
Romeo in the Rain #743
Lion on the Prowl #808
Sydney's Folly #834
Prenuptial Agreement #898
Uncle Daddy #916
Marriage in a Suitcase #949
Timely Matrimony #1030
The Dad Next Door #1108
Carried Away #1438

Silhouette Yours Truly

Husbands Don't Grow on Trees

Harlequin Love & Laughter

Five's a Crowd

Silhouette Books

Baby Fever

KASEY MICHAELS,

the author of more than two dozen books, divides her creative time between writing contemporary romance and Regency novels. Kasey is married and the mother of four; her writing has garnered the Romance Writers of America's Golden Medallion award and *Romantic Times Magazine*'s Best Regency trophy.

Chapter One

Ashley Dawson's Monday began pretty much like any other Monday. She met it reluctantly, having had just enough leisure on her weekend off to want to believe, if just for a moment, that the independently wealthy had the right idea—working for your living could be a real drag.

At least on Monday mornings.

She slept through her alarm, burnt the toast, and belatedly realized she'd put her whites in the washer but never transferred them to the dryer. As for the rest of her wash? Well, that didn't bear thinking about at the moment, not when she'd spent the weekend painting her kitchen.

Not that it mattered. She didn't have to wear a uniform, but most of the staff did, donning either Easter Egg–colored scrubs or white slacks and colored tops.

Well, not her. Not today.

She pulled into the local gas station, her three-year-old car running on fumes, spilled gasoline on her new white leather sneakers as she worked the pump, and the minimart inside the station was out of her favorite cinnamon-and-raisin bagels.

The delays in her usual routine also meant she had missed that narrow window of opportunity that stood between a fairly pleasant ride to work and playing stop-and-go behind a dozen school busses loading slow-walking kids who were probably looking forward to their Monday as much as Ashley was at the moment.

Her mind filled with super-bills, patient schedules, postings left over from the weekend, and the certainty that Cindy Schmidt would be even later arriving at the Flatrock Medical Center than she, Ashley barely had time to do her usual eyes-left glare at the sign on the vacant property along Hamilton Boulevard. But the glare and the muttered disparaging words had become as much a part of her morning these past months as brushing her teeth.

With at least one part of her routine accomplished without incident, she then put on her turn signal and entered the parking lot of the Flatrock Medical Center.

She parked in her usual spot, slid her long, jeans-clad legs out of the car, pushed back a thick lock of chin-length russet hair the wind had found. And went on full alert.

She was no longer Ashley Dawson, bad Monday person. As of this moment, she was Ashley Dawson, Office Manager and still sometimes Medical Assistant. She jogged toward the urgent-care entrance to the large building, as there was a woman standing outside, wearing a worried frown and holding a small child wrapped in a blanket.

Just another Monday morning.

"Cindy, I'll watch the reception area while you take your break, okay?" Ashley said once the morning rush seemed to be over. It was only ten-thirty, and they'd already checked in over forty patients, which was pretty typical for a Monday. There'd be fifty more before she left at five-thirty, turning over the reins to the evening personnel.

Cindy, never one who had to be asked twice when the question was "Do you want to take a break?" was out of the office in a heartbeat. Two seconds later, all five telephone lines began to ring, and Ashley and the rest of the reception area staff were back at it, handling calls that ranged from patients wanting to schedule appointments to some of the medical staff calling in for messages, and everything in between.

So many doctors, so many patients. So much activity, from the expected to the truly bizarre. All of it filtered through this one reception area...this one gateway, this portal that was the nerve center of the entire operation.

And Ashley Dawson, at the fairly tender age of twenty-four, was in charge of it all. Major General of the entire Flatrock Medical Center. The person who made all the madness work.

Being the office manager in a freestanding medical center with a staff of twenty doctors, some of them with their own specialities, including same-day surgeries, some working the urgent-care facility that was also a part of the practice, all of them with their own quirks and demands, their own egos and temperaments, was rather like juggling eggs with your eyes closed. Sometimes you made a great omelette...and sometimes you just ended up with yolk all over your face.

Ashley loved every fast-paced, invigorating, maddening, frustrating, rewarding moment of it.

With two patients on hold, a phone stuck to her ear, the sound of a crying child coming to her through the dividing glass she opened with her free hand as a patient walked up to the reception desk, Ashley was in her element, calmly, efficiently, and pleasantly making sense out of controlled chaos. And then she saw the blood.

"Janie, I'm on hold with Admissions at the hospital, trying to get a bed for Mr. Samuelson. Handle it, will you? Theresa, take the calls on hold—they're both to schedule appointments with Rheumatology. I've got blood out here."

Crying children got your attention. Complainers got your attention. But nothing got your attention faster than blood. In this case, a bloody handkerchief wrapped around a hand held up by...*wow—hell-O, Monday!*

Ashley held up one finger, wordlessly telling the man—the tall, tanned, green-eyed hunk of gorgeous—to stay where he was, then walked around the reception desk, grabbing a disposable towel and one-time use ice bag as she went.

"What happened? May I see, please?" she asked pleasantly, leading him to a seat, just wanting to hear him talk, judge his condition. As she sat him down she gave him a quick once-over, ignoring the gorgeous part and concentrating on whether or not the guy was going to hit the floor any time soon. The bigger they were, she knew, the harder they fell, and the sight of blood seemed to turn more than a few rugged he-men into falling oaks.

He was an obedient sort. He sat down. He unwrapped the handkerchief, revealing a pretty nasty gash across his palm. And he told her what happened. "I wasn't watching where I was going, and tripped over something. My hand landed on a sharp bit of masonry. I'm figuring about three stitches?"

Ashley nodded, wrapping his hand in the disposable towel, preparing the ice bag and carefully placing it over the towel. She tried not to notice that he had a fairly deep, faintly husky and damned sexy voice. The sort of voice that could get away with a lame come-on line like, "Have we met before?" and have her babbling back that they surely hadn't, because she most certainly would have remembered.

So she kept her gaze concentrated on his hand, not the fact that she was touching his wrist, feeling the tingling prickle of the dark blond hairs on his tanned forearms.

She couldn't look up, couldn't take a chance on encountering those laughing green eyes, not if she wanted to remain a professional, objective observer. "Maybe four, as that's rather nasty. And a tetanus shot, of course, unless you're up-to-date?"

"I'm good there, as I tend to get my share of scrapes and cuts on the job. Do you need my insurance information?"

Okay. So she had to look up, couldn't keep talking to his bandaged left hand. "Are you right-handed?"

"Yes, thank goodness." His smile was wide, unaffected. Just as if he didn't know he was the handsomest man in creation or that her entire mind seemed to be turning to mush as she looked at him.

"Good...um...that's *good*," she told him, wondering if the lock of thick sable brown hair that had fallen down onto his forehead bothered him and what he'd do if she reached up, brushed it back for him...

What was *wrong* with her?

She gave a quick shake of her head, got herself back under control. "We'll have a room in the urgent-care center open in a few minutes, and since you're in no danger of bleeding to death in the next ten minutes, I'll bring you our information sheet. You can fill it out and then I'll take it when I bring you back into a room."

"Fine, Ms....?"

"Dawson. Ashley Dawson," she said, then got up, somehow made her way back behind the reception desk for a clipboard and pen.

"Hubba-hubba," Janie whispered, putting her hand over the telephone receiver as Ashley leaned across her to retrieve a pen. "I can't see past the bandage. Is there a ring on that third finger, left hand?"

"Down, girl," Ashley told her quietly, "the man's a patient."

"And I'm a patient woman," Janie responded cheekily. "I can wait until he ditches the wife, then whisks me off to romantic Bora Bora."

Ashley grinned as Janie, fifty years old and happily married for twenty-five years, wriggled her eyebrows at her. "That's it. This whole office is now officially switched to decaf coffee," she said, then took the clipboard and pen to Gorgeous before getting back to the ringing phones.

Not that she forgot him, forgot that he was sitting directly across from the reception desk, and not that she could fight the feeling that he was staring at her, watching her every move, and enjoying himself mightily while he was at it.

When he lifted the clipboard, signaling that he was done filling out the short information form, she nodded in his direction, then retrieved the clipboard, telling him once more than they'd be with him shortly.

Her smile still in place, she began reading the information sheet as she headed for her computer, then sat down heavily, unable to believe what she was reading.

"Figures," she muttered under her breath. "After all, it *is* Monday."

She was just entering the last bits of information into the computer when Cindy returned from her break.

"Ashley!" The young woman's excited whisper followed Ashley as she stood up, headed for the copy machine. "Janie told me to look into the reception area. Did you *see* him? The long, lean one in all that denim and dust? He's…well, he's a…"

"A god?" Ashley supplied sourly, photocopying the insurance card Gorgeous had handed her.

"Yes! And that smile. It's…it's…"

"Irresistible?" Ashley gritted out from between clenched teeth.

"Uh-huh. Those *eyes* of his, they're so...so..."

"The word you're searching for, Cindy, is green. I'd noticed. Now excuse me, okay? I've got to take our smiling green-eyed god back to Examine-two."

"You lucky dog!"

"Yeah, right. I only hope Dr. Childs has a really dull needle ready for him." Ashley walked out into the reception area once more and, with all professionalism—and not a hint of her usual smile—said, "Mr. Callahan? We're ready for you now. Please follow me."

Ashley had suffered through worse Mondays, but not in recent history.

It wasn't the work, the sheer load of it, because she liked her job, enjoyed her career. What bothered her, what had haunted her most of the day, was the fact that she hadn't been able to divorce the professional Ashley from the woman who had wanted to grab hold of Logan Callahan's light blue denim work shirt and shake him until his teeth rattled.

Or maybe kiss him.

She tried to banish both equally stupid thoughts as she finally turned everything over to the night staff and walked out into the sun that wouldn't go down for three more hours. She'd go home, eat something sinfully fattening and totally devoid of roughage or essential nutrients, put her whites in the dryer, and find some sappy movie on cable. Something that would make her cry, because she felt like she needed a good cry.

Theresa always complained that "all the good ones are married." Ashley could amend that statement now, to say that all the handsome, knee-melting ones were lousy, no-good, moneygrubbing, bottom-line oriented, heartless sons of...

Ashley clutched her keys tightly in her hand as she stopped in the middle of the parking lot and looked at the man sitting on the hood of a dusty dark burgundy Mercedes sedan. The really big model, the one with the teardrop headlights. The kind of car moneygrubbing heartless business types probably owned by the dozens, even if this one looked as if it hadn't seen a car wash shop in months.

She narrowed her eyes, glared at Logan Callahan as he just sat there, one construction boot resting on the fender, the other bent at the knee as he held onto it with his uninjured hand. The denim shirt with the sleeves rolled up to the elbows, the tight blue jeans he'd poured himself in that morning. The lock of hair still blowing against his forehead. The natural tan, the smile on his face, the beginnings of a five o'clock shadow on his smooth cheeks, the twinkle in his Irish green eyes. The man was probably illegal in at least three states.

She walked past him, heading for her own car, which happened to be parked right next to his. At the last moment she stopped again, spared him a look, indulged herself in a question. "What are you doing here, Mr. Callahan? We released you hours ago." She turned, stuck the key in the lock. "Don't you have a home?"

She sensed that he'd eased away from his car and now stood behind her. "I'm just trying to figure out what went wrong in there, Ms. Ashley Dawson," he said, and she had to turn around once more—soon she'd be spinning like a top—and ask him what he was talking about, as nothing had "gone wrong" in there. He'd been seen, treated, told to return in a week to have the stitches removed or see his own doctor.

"What went—what do you mean?" was all she could muster, which was pretty weak when she considered that she usually believed herself to be at least marginally articulate.

He leaned against the front door of the Mercedes—couldn't the man stand up without help?—and shrugged his shoulders. "I'm not sure. I just know you met me with a smile, then turned cold as February once I'd handed you my forms and insurance card. You were nice to everyone else—I watched—but I didn't need an ice bag anymore. You were freezing me straight through to the bone. And," he ended, his smile suggesting several sinful earthly dleights, "I couldn't help myself. I had to stick around and find out why. Oh, I did go grab a sandwich, in case you're worrying that I'm giddy from loss of blood. Did anyone ever tell you that your eyes are exactly the color of horse chestnuts?"

She'd been right. The guy was great, even with the corniest line. Right about now Janie would be giggling inanely and rattling off her phone number. Ashley inspected her ring of keys, unable to keep her fingers from fidgeting. "Horse chestnuts? Well, that's a new one."

"I can do better," Logan told her, "but I'm in pain, you know."

Ashley lifted her head, looked at him intently as her sympathies were aroused in spite of her dislike—

please let this feeling she was experiencing be dislike. "Really? Well, that's your own fault, you know. We told you to go home and take the painkillers, didn't we? The local anesthetic only lasts so long, and then the feeling can come back with a vengeance." She motioned toward his bandaged hand. "It isn't throbbing, is it? The wound was pretty dirty."

"Ah, the way to the woman's heart. I always heard it was flowers. Now I know better. If I whimper, will you let me take you to dinner?"

"I don't think so, no," she answered, wondering why she wasn't getting into her car, heading home to a dinner she'd eat while standing at the sink. Silly question....

"I didn't mean right now, Ms. Dawson," he told her, spreading his hands to indicate that he knew he wasn't dressed for dinner. Actually, he looked like a man who'd been playing in dirt piles most of the day. That he could still be handsome as sin really rankled Ashley.

"And I didn't mean *ever*, Mr. Callahan," she said firmly, then dropped her keys on the macadam. "Damn," she muttered as she bent down, then stood up again quickly, rubbing at her forehead, as he had bent down at the same time, causing a mild collision.

He handed her the key ring. "I'm sorry. That wasn't my smoothest move," he told her. "Look, could we start over?"

"Start over?" Ashley repeated, her hand trembling as she took the keys from him, shoved them into her pocket so that they wouldn't fall again. "I didn't think we'd *started* at all."

His smile started slow, lazily spread to include his eyes, the small laugh lines that crinkled around those eyes. "No? Perhaps I started without you, Ms. Dawson. I only know I came into your office hurting like hell, walked up to the desk, and ten seconds later I forgot I'd been injured. They ought to bottle that smile of yours. It's better than any painkiller. Except that I haven't seen that smile directed at me in—" he paused, looked down at the gold Rolex on his left wrist, "—five hours and thirty-six minutes. I think it's past time for another dose."

Ashley cocked her head to one side, looked up at him in amazement. "Aren't you the least bit embarrassed, saying things like that?"

He grinned, shook his head. "I don't think so, no," he admitted, pulling a crushed Phillies baseball cap from his back pocket and pulling it down low over his eyes. All his movements were slow, almost lazy, and yet somehow efficient. He was fascinating, in so many ways. All of them probably dangerous, especially to a woman who despised the ground he built on.

Still, if she passed up this chance to talk to him, to tell him what she thought? Would she hate herself in the morning if she didn't grab at the opportunity to nail the insufferable man's hide to the barn door? Would she hate herself more if she did?

She shrugged her shoulders, sighed audibly. "Your address is in Philadelphia, so I'm assuming you've got a hotel room here in Allentown?"

"I'm at the Sheraton Jetport, near the airport," he answered, still leaning against the car door, although she noticed a new alertness in his eyes even as they were shadowed by the baseball cap.

"Down boy," she warned him, shaking her head again. "I only asked because you'll need a shower and change of clothes before dinner, right? I know I do. All in all, it's been a long day. That said, if your offer of dinner is still open, I can meet you at the Sheraton in about ninety minutes. Dinner, Mr. Callahan. That's all."

"What else could there be, Ms. Dawson?" he asked, pushing himself away from the car and tipping his cap to her before moving to the driver's side of the Mercedes. "I'll meet you in the lobby. You may not recognize me without the dirt, so I'll be the one with the rose between my teeth, okay?"

She couldn't help herself. She laughed out loud. "Just be careful with the thorns, Mr. Callahan. I'm off-duty."

"Dinner, Mom," Ashley said, trying to put on panty hose and hold the cordless phone to her ear at the same time. "*Dinner*. In a public place. What could go wrong?"

She winced as her mother's voice shot back across the wires. "What could go wrong? Ashley, Ashley, Ashley, have I been that remiss in my lessons? Don't talk to strangers. I did tell you that, right? Don't take candy, don't talk. I distinctly remember saying something like that."

"And I distinctly remembering hearing it," Ashley said as she stood up, pulling the panty hose to her waist, then walked to her closet to pick out a dress to wear to dinner. "But I'm not ten years old, and Logan Callahan isn't some nutcase serial killer. Besides, I just couldn't pass up the opportunity to give him a piece of my mind.''

"But you'll be polite?"

Ashley took the phone away from her ear, stared at it for a moment before putting it back. "Polite? Mom, the guy is tearing down the Sandler house to put up a *factory*. How am I supposed to be polite when I call him a moneygrubbing heathen without a scrap of…of…well, whatever he should have a scrap of, he doesn't!''

"Decency?" Lindsay Dawson volunteered. "I think you mean scrap of decency. And, my darling, if you think that badly of the man, how can you possibly still tell me I shouldn't worry? I'm calling your sister.''

"Mom, don't—'' Ashley began quickly, just before the dial tone sounded in her ear. "Great,'' she grumbled, throwing the phone onto the bed. "That's just great.''

Five minutes later, as Ashley stood in front of the full-length mirror, inspecting her hastily thrown on outfit of lime green brushed denim skirt and matching cotton flowered blouse, the phone rang again.

She picked it up, pushed the Talk button. "Look, Mary, I don't need a chaperone, I'm not crazy, and Mom doesn't have to call from King of Prussia to have my baby sister check up on me. It's just a dinner, for crying out loud. Now, if you don't mind—''

"Ms. Dawson?"

"Oh, Gawd,'' Ashley groaned, collapsing onto the side of the bed as she recognized Logan Callahan's voice. "How did you get my number?"

The lazy, husky baritone purred through the lines. "You're in the book, Ms. Dawson. A. Dawson. You really shouldn't do that, you know. The initial is a dead giveaway that you're a woman alone who doesn't want to look like she's a woman alone. Who's Mary?"

Ashley ran her free hand through her hair, pushing its blunt-cut length behind her ear. "Mary is my sister—the one beeping right now on my other line, I'm sure, and, no, if I ignore her she won't go away. She'll just drive over here, flags waving, and I'll never get rid of her. Have you called to cancel?" The thought did not appeal, not that she'd admit as much to him.

"Cancel? No." She could hear the hint of amusement in his tone, and pictured his smile, his laughing eyes. What about her amused him so much, damn it? "I only thought that, seeing how much road construction there is here at the airport, perhaps we could meet somewhere else. I wouldn't want you to have to deal with all the detours and traffic. I'm considerate that way, you know."

"And modest with it all," Ashley shot back, already looking at her watch, deciding that he was right. At this time of night, the highways would be clogged for miles in each direction.

"Okay," she said, nodding even though he couldn't see her. She searched her brain for a restaurant that would be an equal distance between the hotel and her own apartment. "Do you have a pencil and paper handy? There's a small bar and restaurant in a shopping center that shouldn't be crowded on a Monday night. They make a mean chili, and great charcoal-grilled, open-faced steak sandwiches. I can give you directions."

"Sounds great," he said after she'd quickly given him the directions. "Guess they serve all kinds of beer, huh? If I don't take one of these pain pills, do you think I could have one?"

"You haven't taken a pain pill?" She tried to decide whether he thought himself to be some macho-man or if he'd just been too lazy to pour himself a glass of water and open the pill bottle.

"No, I thought I might need a clear head tonight, Ashley," he said, the good humor back in his voice. "After all, I still want to find out why you hate me."

"I don't—oh, darn it, Mary's trying to beep in again. I have to go. I'll meet you at seven, all right?"

Without giving him time to answer, she pressed the Call-waiting button in time to hear her sister saying, "I don't know, Paul, she's not answering. Maybe we should go on over there?"

"No!" Ashley called into the receiver, gaining her sister's attention. "No, Mary, you and Paul definitely should *not* come on over here. I'm going to dinner with a patient. Nothing more, nothing less. Lord, we gotta put Mom on a leash, Mare, or she's going to be running our lives until we're pushing our walkers in the old folks home."

Her sister's soft laughter came to her over the phone lines. "You know how it is, Ash. Mom lost her baby to marriage only four months—shhh, Paul! Yes, yes, four months, two weeks and three days ago. Honestly, some husbands!" Then she giggled, and Ashley rolled her eyes, knowing Paul had most probably come up behind Mary and was kissing her.

"Anyway, Ash, Mom has one married daughter now, and one who's been independent since she was old enough to tie her own shoes. That's you, Ash. Don't blame her if she gets a little proprietorial once in a while. Besides, you always said you don't date your patients. It's not professional, or something like that."

"He's not a regular patient, Mary, just a walk-in emergency. And since when do you start quoting me back to me? What else did Mom tell you?"

"Only that you're going to dinner at the Jetport and that if you're not home by ten Paul and I are supposed to saddle up and go rescue you."

Ashley seriously considered leaving that statement stand, then decided against it. Lying to her sister, even by omission, just wasn't something she could do. Besides, they'd probably hunt her down anyway.

"Change of plans, Mare. We're meeting at that small beef and ale place you and I went to last week. And, if I'm not home by ten, my dear, I'll be home at eleven, so you and Paul just have yourselves a nice evening—and you might want to take your phone off the hook in case Mom decides to call again."

"Good point," her sister agreed. "So, tell me about this guy, okay? Is he handsome?"

"Unbearably handsome," Ashley told her, carrying the phone with her as she headed into the living room, pulled a light jacket from the closet. "Tall, dark brown hair, greener than green eyes, legs as long as—well, long—and a killer smile. And, since you're going to ask anyway, his name is Logan Callahan. *Callahan,* Mare. Sound familiar?"

"Callahan? *Callahan!* Ohmigawd, Ash, not Callahan and Son?"

"One and the same, and I think we're talking 'and son' here," Ashley told her, searching on the couch for her keys, finding them slipped behind one of the half-dozen throw pillows. "Should be an interesting evening, don't you think?"

"I'll keep the phone on the hook and start collecting bail money," Mary said, sighing. "I know you, big sister, and you and your pals in the Historical Committee been busy building up a head of steam on this one for months. Are you going to ask him why he's doing it?"

"Sure am," Ashley told her as she walked toward the front door of her apartment. "I'm going to nail him to the wall about his greedy corporate irresponsibility. Right after I bring him back here, toss him down on the carpet, squirt whipped cream all over his body and shamelessly seduce him. Night, Mare."

She laughed as she hit the Disconnect button, tossed the phone across the room onto the couch, and made it out of the apartment before the phone began ringing again.

Chapter Two

"This had better be good, Logan. It's just past seven here—that's in the *a.m.*, son, in case you've forgotten—and I was out until three, wining and dining our newest clients. Hopefully our newest clients."

Logan sat back on the hotel bed, his long legs crossed in front of him on the mattress as he hit the Mute button on the television remote.

He'd phoned Ryan Callahan on a whim, a small happy thought he hadn't quite formulated in his mind, but it definitely had all the hallmarks of a good idea. As long as he could make his father think the whole thing was his idea, that is.

He smiled into the receiver. "And a great big sloppy, sentimental hello to you, too, Dad. And, now that I think about it, I guess it isn't all that important. Bye."

"Logan, hang up that phone and I'll cut off your allowance!"

"My allowance?" Logan laughed out loud. "Dad, I haven't had an allowance since I was fifteen and started working with you. But, then, you're old now, so you probably don't remember. So, how'd you find Tokyo?"

"Fairly easily. It's still about seven thousand miles west of Philadelphia," Ryan Callahan told his son, and Logan could hear his father coming more awake, and most definitely more alert. "So, what's going on? You're in Allentown, right? Trouble on the site?"

Now here was a dilemma. If Logan said no, which was true, he'd be heading back to Philadelphia tomorrow morning. He didn't want to do that, not when he'd met Ashley Dawson, wanted to get to know Ashley Dawson.

"Well, there's a couple of small things..." he began slowly, then looked up at the ceiling, waiting for lightning to strike straight through the building. He decided not to lie, and went for sympathy instead. That always worked as the twenty-seven-year-old and only son of Ryan Callahan, ruthless businessman and doting, almost overprotective dad. "I tripped over something on the site, sliced up my hand."

"Bad? Am I to hop the next plane, come home and kiss it all better?" Ryan was playing it light, but Logan could hear the concern in his father's voice.

He decided to go easy on him.

"Very funny, Dad. Four stitches. Nothing major, and I'd be able to play the violin once it healed, if I could have played the violin in the first place. Except you never sent me for violin lessons, did you? Just another life experience I've missed in my headlong rush to grow up to be just like Daddy,'' Logan told him, tongue-in-cheek. ''But it did mean I spent most of the day in some local emergency center, so I didn't get to conduct more than a cursory inspection of the site. And the bulldozers start clearing the ground next week. That said, I think I'll stick around a few more days, since there's nothing pressing back at the office, at least nothing Prescott can't handle.''

''And you're asking my permission? Why don't I believe that?''

''Probably because I'm not,'' Logan replied, clicking off the television as he noticed the time on the clock next to the bed. His movements were slow, unhurried, not a single motion wasted. His father always said his son reminded him of molasses pouring through water—getting where he wanted to go, but never in a hurry. ''I just thought I'd check up on the old man, see if he needed the benefit of my expertise.''

''Yeah. That'll be the day,'' Ryan Callahan growled, then chuckled low in his throat. ''I miss you, Logan. With luck, I'll be back in the States by the middle or end of next week, the Hoshi contract in my pocket.''

''That's my dad,'' Logan told him cheerfully. ''My hero.''

There was a pause at the other end of the line, then Ryan spoke again, his tone thoughtful. ''You know, you should have come over here with me, Logan. How long has it been since you've had a real vacation?''

Bingo! And there it was. Just what Logan had wanted to hear. He had his opening. And, knowing there were only so many opportunities that fell into a person's lap, he'd recognized this one at once. "Vacation? I'm not familiar with the word. Perhaps you could spell it for me?"

"Point taken," Ryan said, and Logan thought he could hear the gears in his father's head turning. He hoped they'd slow down soon, settle in the right slots. "All right. Finish up at the Allentown site, then take a week off."

"A whole week? Gee whiz, Daddy, thanks. What *will* I do with all that time? Seven whole days, gosh," Logan drawled, checking his reflection in the mirror, carelessly pushing fingers through his thick, always-in-need-of-a-haircut shag of sable brown hair.

"Nobody likes a smart-ass, son, remember that. Okay. Two weeks. But that's it. And it's only because I'm probably going to wrap up the Hoshi deal tomorrow, then get in some sightseeing. You could still fly out, join me?"

Logan picked up a pen, began tapping it against the receiver. "What's that, Dad? I think we're losing the satellite, or whatever."

"What's that racket? Speak up, Logan, I can't hear you. I said, come to Tokyo. You could probably get a flight out of Philadelphia tomorrow night."

"Yup, the line's breaking up, Dad. I could barely hear anything you said that time. Before I lose you...thanks for the offer of a vacation, and I gratefully accept. I haven't hit a Florida beach since my last spring break in college. You have fun, too. Ciao!"

"That's *sayonara*, you idiot!" his dad shouted into the phone, and Logan had to put his hand over the receiver so that Ryan wouldn't hear his snort of laughter. "Ah, the hell with it," his dad said at last, "I'm going back to bed."

Logan looked at the receiver for a moment after his dad hung up, then grinned at himself as he was reflected in the mirror.

"You're a bad man, Logan Callahan. A bad, bad man. And now you have a good ten days of sweet, unfettered freedom stretching out in front of you. So, sport, what're you going to do now that you've conned your father?"

He grabbed his baseball cap, brought it down low over his eyes, looked into the mirror once more and addressed his own reflection. "Well, sir, I'm going to go have dinner with Ashley Dawson, then drive that gorgeous, provocative woman nuts for the next ten days. If I'm lucky."

Logan found the small beef and ale restaurant without a problem, arriving only ten minutes late which, for him, was pretty close to being unconscionably early.

He parked the dusty Mercedes next to Ashley's sparkling clean compact car, crossed the parking lot with his easy, long-legged strides, and pulled open the thick wooden door that opened into a narrow hallway dark enough to make him pause until his eyes adjusted to the dimness.

The sounds of a jukebox playing some vintage Garth Brooks led him toward the right, and the barroom, where Ashley sat on a high stool at one end of the long bar, sipping a soda and glancing at her watch.

It would figure that she'd be a clock-watcher, the sort of efficient person capable of running an office, the sort of impatient person who actually thought seven o'clock actually *meant* seven o'clock. He'd have to get her to relax....

She spied him in the mirror above the bar and turned on the stool, watching him walk toward her. Her lovely face was set in tight lines, just as it had been since he'd first turned over his personal information to her, with no trace of the softness of her, the humanness of her that she'd shared with every other patient, with her co-workers.

Intriguing. Very intriguing. Logan liked everybody. And everybody pretty much liked him.

This woman looked like her idea of a good time would be boiling him in oil.

And yet...and yet? Was he kidding himself to believe there was also some interest lurking in her big brown eyes, some small bit of encouragement to be gleaned from the way she had finally given in to him, agreed to meet him for dinner?

"Hi," he said, tipping back his hat as he slid onto the bar stool next to hers, wrapping his long legs around the thing. He could smell her perfume, and it smelled good, giving him an appetite that didn't have much to do with charcoal-grilled steak or chili. "Am I late?"

She leaned her elbows against the bar, looked at him closely. "If you marked time like the rest of the world, yes. But I have the feeling that you run on your own clock. Am I right?"

Logan told the approaching bartender that he'd have a glass of whatever the guy had on tap, then grinned at Ashley. "Know my dad, do you?" he quipped, then laughed as she frowned, looked confused for a moment.

"Um...there's a small table over there," she said, pointing to a booth on the other side of the long, narrow room. "Unless you'd rather go in the back room, away from the bar?"

"This will be fine," he answered, picking up her soda and his iced glass of draft, then allowing her to lead the way to the booth fashioned of two rustic-looking black-painted wooden seats with high backs, the seats separated by a thin sliver of table.

He watched her slide into one side of the booth, admiring her long legs beneath the short denim skirt, happy to see they were as perfect as he'd imagined them earlier when they'd been covered by her jeans, then slipped onto the opposite seat.

She looked at him for a moment, then bent her head, busied herself in shredding the damp napkin stuck to the bottom of her sweating glass.

He made a small business out of looking at the booth, as if measuring it. "Are you sure this booth is big enough for three of us?"

That brought her head up. "Three of us?" Then she shook her head, smiled wryly. "No, Mary won't be joining us. Not unless she wants me to tell her new husband about the time she dyed her hair purple."

A waitress came over to take their order, and Logan indicated that Ashley should order for him. She was as good as her word, ordering them chili and steaks, not even hesitating to agree when the waitress suggested raw onions on the steak sandwiches.

Obviously not an indication that this was to be any sort of romantic evening.

"How's your hand?" Ashley asked once the waitress had gone. "That was a pretty nasty cut."

Logan looked down at his hand, mildly surprised to see the bandage. He'd all but forgotten about the cut. "I think I'll live," he said, taking a sip of cold beer, feeling its sharp tang against his tongue. "You've got a nice facility, you know, if a bit large and confusing. I wasn't sure I was in the right place at first."

That did it. A nice, easy inquiry into her job, her place of employment. She sat back against the back of the booth, her posture more relaxed than it had been since he'd first walked into the restaurant.

"We do have a lot going on," she conceded, and the smile was back, the smile he'd seen this morning, the one that had started this strange, tight coil low in his belly. "We have three separate specialities sharing our space, two family physicians, along with a same-day surgery and the emergency walk-in clinic. It keeps us hopping."

"And you're in charge." He didn't ask the question, but stated it as fact. "I was watching, remember? Everyone's eyes went to you, everyone's questions were directed to you."

"You notice a lot for a man who only spent a few minutes in the reception area," Ashley said, shifting slightly in the booth, her nervousness back.

"Enough to notice that something about my information sheet pretty much wiped the smile from your face." He waited until the waitress put two steaming bowls of chili in front of them, then asked, "Are you going to tell me why?"

"Moving a little faster now, aren't you?" Ashley made a great business out of opening the cellophane-wrapped crackers, crumbling them into her chili.

Logan waited, a patient man, and a man wondering why he'd compared her eyes to horse chestnuts. She looked more like Bambi right now, momentarily caught in headlights.

She shrugged her shoulders, sighed rather soulfully, then wiped the cracker crumbs off her fingers and looked at him levelly. "All right. I thought it could wait until we'd eaten, but I guess there's no reason to pretend this is a social evening." She leaned forward, as if for emphasis. "Because it isn't, you know."

Logan hesitated as he lifted his spoon to his mouth, cocked an eyebrow at her. "It's not? Well, there go all my hopes and dreams—although the onions, and this chili, were pretty much dead giveaways anyway."

"You're a very infuriating man, do you know that?" Ashley complained, grabbing his packet of crackers and ripping it open with enough force to send both crackers skidding across the table and onto the floor. She glared at him accusingly. "*Now* look what you made me do!"

"You didn't want them anyway," Logan pointed out, knowing he was infuriating her, but rather liking the way her cheeks colored when she was angry. "Now, tell me why you hate me. I know it isn't just on general principles."

"It could be, Callahan, quite easily," Ashley retorted sharply, then let her shoulders slump. "I'm sorry. That was mean."

"No, it wasn't," Logan corrected, impulsively reaching across the narrow table and taking her hand, squeezing it for a moment. Her skin was warm, and soft, the sort of hand that was washed often, then cared for with sweet-smelling creams. "I haven't exactly been on my best behavior. I promise to be good from now on, Scout's honor. Now, why don't you tell me what's on your mind?"

She pushed the bowl of chili away from her, obviously not wanting to speak and eat at the same time. "It's your name. Callahan. I've been cursing it for so long, I guess I had some sort of juvenile, knee-jerk reaction to seeing it today on your information sheet."

Logan nodded, signaling that he understood, while not understanding at all. "My name. Okay. So you have an aversion to Callahans. What happened? Were you frightened by one as a child?"

She glared at him accusingly. "I thought you said you were going to be nice."

"Sorry."

"Yes, well, you should be. I haven't had the easiest day, you know."

Logan didn't know when last he'd enjoyed himself so much. "And this would be my fault?"

Ashley opened her mouth, probably to curse him—which he knew he deserved—and then suddenly plopped both elbows on the table and started to laugh. "Do you *hear* us, Callahan? Amazing, isn't it, how two people who don't even know each other can find so much to argue about."

Logan smiled, slowly, easing his way into his own appreciation of their predicament. "We do seem to be striking sparks off one another," he agreed, then couldn't resist adding, "not that I'm to blame. Except that I'm a Callahan. There is that."

"Yes, there is that." Ashley sobered. "Okay, here it is, quickly, before you can interrupt. Have you ever heard of Sandler House?"

Logan lifted the spoon to his mouth once more, then hesitated as Ashley looked at him. "What? Oh—I'm allowed to answer? I thought I wasn't supposed to interrupt. Or eat, now that I think about it. But, to answer your question, no, I've never heard of Sandler House. Should I have?"

"Since your stupid company is ripping Sandler House down to build a stupid factory, *yes,* Callahan, you should have," Ashley answered, sitting back as the waitress delivered their steak sandwiches.

Logan smiled up at the waitress, a woman who also was looking at him as if he'd just burrowed out from under a rock. "Could I have some steak sauce, please?" he asked, wondering when it was he'd begun to have such a negative effect on those of the female persuasion.

"They're tearing down Sandler House?" the waitress asked Ashley, ignoring Logan's request. "I didn't know that."

"Oh, yes," Ashley told the woman, moving over on the bench seat so that the waitress could sit down beside her.

"Okay, that's good. Talk to her," Logan said,

amused at this informality, "and I'll listen. Maybe then I'll finally get to know why you hate me."

The waitress looked from Ashley to Logan and then back again. "You hate him, hon? Why?" She leaned closer to Ashley, whispered just a little too loudly not to have Logan overhear: "Haven't you noticed how *gorgeous* he is?"

"Well, thank you, ma'am, I appreciate that. As to why she hates me—so far, we think it's my name. Callahan. I don't know. Maybe she can't spell it? It's simple enough, *C-a-l-l—*"

"Be quiet and eat your dinner," Ashley and the waitress said at the same time, before Ashley took a sip of soda and launched into an explanation—if a coherent one was possible at this point, which Logan was beginning to doubt.

Still, it looked like Ashley was going to give it the old college try. "I'm Ashley, and he's Logan Callahan. He's an architect," she began, hooking a thumb in Logan's direction, her tone indicating that he couldn't be more damned if she'd said, "he's a thrill killer."

The waitress nodded as if she understood, then frowned. "Nope. I don't get it, hon. What does he have to do with Sandler House? Oh, and I'm Ruth."

"Hi, Ruth," Logan ventured, waggling his fingertips at her as he inspected the slab of open-face Delmonico steak, trying to figure out the logistics involved in folding it into the toasted bun and then getting all that meat, lettuce, tomato and bun—he'd pushed the onion to one side—into his mouth at one time. It looked like a lot of work.

"You know that tract of land bordering Hamilton

Boulevard, Ruth?'' Ashley asked, ignoring both her meal and Logan. "Right down the street from the Burger King restaurant?"

"Not nice to mention the competition when you're eating someone's food,'' Logan slid in, then held up his hands in surrender as Ashley's Bambi eyes narrowed to dangerous-looking slits.

"I know the spot,'' Ruth said, nodding. "They're building a huge telecommunications center or something there, aren't they?''

"That's it. Great big telecommunications center. A real feat of inspired architecture, too, Ruth. And I should know. But not to hear Ashley tell it,'' Logan put in, considering himself to be a braver man than he'd previously believed, daring to interrupt yet again. "She calls it a factory. But you didn't hear that, Ruth. I'm eating, see?'' he ended, taking a huge bite of his sandwich.

"Don't take such big bites,'' Ashley warned him, as if used to being in charge of everyone's life, even his, and he wanted to lean across the table, slide his hand behind her neck, and pull her close for a kiss. Which surprised him. He didn't know he liked bossy women.

Ruth waved her hands at both of them. "But Sandler House sits back from the road, doesn't it? Can't they just build around it?''

At this statement, Logan choked on a bit of steak, made a rather large point out of reaching a hand over his shoulder to pound on his own back. "Build... build *around* it? Oh, that's good, Ruth. That's really good.''

"Chew your food before you stick your foot in

your mouth," Ashley warned him before ignoring
him once more. "That's what I think, Ruth," she
said, obviously warming to her subject. "And so
does the Historical Society. It's a large plot of
ground. Why *not* build around it?"

Logan closed his eyes, trying to conjure up a mental picture of the tract of land he'd walked that morning—or at least tried to walk, until he'd taken his
fall, cut his hand. Yes, he could see it now, in his
mind's eye. A three-story fieldstone house off in the
distance, probably an old farmhouse. He even remembered that he'd been vaguely surprised to see it
there, as he hadn't thought it had appeared on any
of the plans he'd okayed when they crossed his desk
six months earlier.

"The Historical Society?" he then asked, trying
to get Ashley's attention. "Let me guess. Just a wild
stab in the dark, okay? You're a member, aren't
you?"

"Secretary," Ashley said, bristling.

"Hoo-boy," he breathed, draining his glass of
beer, then waiting as the bartender called to Ruth,
telling her to wait on the customers that had just
come into the restaurant. "Tell me something, Ashley. Are you and your fellow members going to be
chaining yourselves together and plopping yourselves down in front of the land movers coming in
next week? Please tell me you're not doing that."

She glared at him, then bent her head, traced a
small pattern on the wooden table top with her index
finger. "I was voted down," she said in a small
voice.

"Well, thank the good Lord for small favors," Logan said, touching the plate holding her steak. "Here, eat. And then you can tell me all about Sandler House, okay? Maybe there's something we can do."

Ten minutes of dedicated talking and eating later, the food was gone and Logan had the full story.

He sat back, tossed his crumpled paper napkin on the remains of his sandwich. "There's nothing I can do."

Ashley opened her mouth, obviously to protest, but he waved a hand at her, cutting her off.

"Look, Ashley. Let's try to be reasonable here. You told me you guys tried for two years to get Sandler House on the National Register. It didn't qualify. You've also told me that the place has been vacant for years, the roof is pretty well shot, the windows are mostly gone and, basically, the place is falling down. Your organization doesn't have the money to renovate, and you can't get a government grant. I don't know, Ashley, but a quick death by bulldozer almost sounds like the kindest thing to do."

"It's not fair," Ashley responded tightly. "We're losing our history left, right and center, Callahan. And all for the almighty dollar. I can't tell you the number of fine old houses that were leveled just because the huge companies now owning the properties didn't want to pay the piddling property taxes on them. We even lost our fort—Fort Deshler. That's where the local people gathered when the Indian attacks began, way back in the 1760s. Now all that's left is a placard on the side of the highway. And for what, Callahan? *Progress?* Please don't tell me you think that's progress."

"No, Ashley, but I do call it inevitable. We can't preserve every last farmhouse, every last building. All right, so ripping down the fort was probably going too far. I'll admit to that one. But this place..."

"Sandler House."

"Right. Sandler House. This place, by your own admission, is just about falling down."

"It could be fixed," she told him in a small voice, avoiding his eyes. "It was a bed-and-breakfast up until about a dozen years ago, when Hamilton Boulevard started growing malls everywhere you turned."

She leaned forward, her brown eyes shining. "You should see the banister, Callahan. I've seen pictures, back from when it was the bed-and-breakfast. It's carved out of a single piece of wood—or at least that's what Bob says."

Logan raised one eyebrow. "Bob?"

She nodded, oblivious to the fact that Logan, against his better judgment, was suddenly wishing her eyes would light up that way when she mentioned *his* name. He spared a moment to hope the gleam in her eyes was for the bannister, not Bob.

"He's one of our members, and the dearest old man," she elaborated for him, not knowing she'd also relegated the inestimable Bob to the unimportant and disposable in Logan's increasingly proprietorial mind. "And there are bullet holes in the mantel over the fireplace in the front room. Bullet holes, Callahan, from when the area was under attack. How do you rip something like that down?"

He was so tempted to answer, "Probably a bulldozer, maybe a strong gust of wind." But he contained himself. "Tell you what, Ashley," he said at
last, reaching into his pocket to pull out money to
pay for their meal. He'd have to leave Ruth a big tip.
After all, she'd called him gorgeous. "I'll be back at
the site tomorrow, all day. If you meet me there on
your lunch hour, we can tour the house together."

She looked at him cautiously, as if weighing his
motives, his sincerity.

She had every right to be cautious, he knew, because there was no way, no way in hell, he could do
anything about Sandler House at this late date. No
way, no how.

"And after we've seen the house?" she asked as
she gathered her purse, a light sweater she'd brought
with her, and led the way to the door. "What then,
Callahan?"

"Good question, Dawson," he countered, then
steered her toward the ice-cream parlor situated beside the steak and ale in the small shopping mall.
"But right now I've got a better one. Do you like
hot fudge?"

Logan lay propped against the headboard of his
bed in the hotel, barely paying attention to the Phillies game on the television screen.

Mostly, he was thinking about Ashley Dawson,
and the way she ate vanilla ice cream. The way she
approached the consumption of hot caramel topping.

This was a woman who enjoyed her food, and he
enjoyed watching her eat it. Especially the caramel,
which she sort of slid around in her mouth, savoring

the taste, sliding the caramel coated spoon into her mouth, then out, then back in again.

He'd nearly broken into a sweat, watching her eat the caramel.

He sat up now, punched at the pillows behind his back, then settled himself once more, wishing he'd brought the site plans with him to the hotel instead of leaving them in the construction trailer at the site.

He wanted to look at those plans again. He wanted to know why Sandler House hadn't appeared on them.

He also wanted to see if the Phillies new pitcher was all he was cracked up to be, but he couldn't seem to pay attention to the game.

Mostly, he wanted Ashley Dawson to stop looking at him so suspiciously and begin smiling at him again. Because he liked her. Prickly, smart, passionate, and nobody's fool. He really, really liked her. He wanted to get to know her. Slowly, leisurely. And without Sandler House standing between them.

"Aw, hell," he said, abandoning the bed as he searched the floor for his sneakers, swearing again as he tried to tie them and forgot that his left hand was giving him hell.

Twenty minutes later, he was walking across the weed-choked Hamilton Boulevard site in the dark, flashlight in hand, fishing in his pocket for the key to the construction trailer.

Once inside, he found the plans he wanted and spread them out on the large table at one end of the trailer.

Nothing. There simply was no indication that Sandler House even existed. That's why he hadn't questioned it—the damn thing hadn't been there.

Now he had questions. He had lots of questions. And no answers.

Because he was the *son* half of Callahan and Son, and Callahan and Son didn't do shoddy work. If the house was there, on the property, it should be here, drawn on the plans. It was as simple as that.

He locked up the construction trailer and returned to his car, picked up the cell phone he kept there, and punched in some numbers.

Ten seconds later, he was telling Barbara Prescott that he was fine, thank you, just fine, he hoped she and the kids were fine, and could he please speak with Rob for a moment.

"Rob?" he said without preamble when the Callahan and Son Vice President picked up the phone. "I'm up in Allentown, remember, checking out the site? Good. Ever hear of Sandler House, Rob? No? Neither did I. I also didn't know we were into demolition. And don't you think it's strange, considering all of that, that we've supposedly recommended knocking down this fine example of early colonial architecture first thing next Monday morning?"

Chapter Three

Ashley woke to the sound of rain pelting against her bedroom window. Ordinarily that wouldn't bother her. But today she was supposed to meet Logan Callahan for lunch. They were supposed to tramp across the fields and inspect Sandler House, a field that would turn into a sea of mud if this rain didn't stop soon.

"I'm *so* lucky," she told herself as she dragged her tired body out of bed and headed for the shower, hoping her new bath soap worked as advertised, immediately waking her up with its sudsing bubbles.

She was tired because she hadn't slept much, finding it rather difficult to get to sleep when every time she closed her eyes she saw Logan Callahan's laughing green eyes, his slow, lazy smile.

He'd gotten to her last night over chili and steak…and ice cream. No question about it.

The only question was, what she was going to do about it?

Okay, so he was gorgeous. Lots of men were gorgeous. Well, not *lots* of men, and most of the gorgeous ones she'd ever seen had been posing in magazine ads. But that wasn't the point. Gorgeous was one thing. Likable was another.

And Logan Callahan was very likable, damn him.

He was the sort of easygoing guy who steamrollered right over you while seeming not to do a thing, make a move in your direction. The sort of guy who agreed with everything you said while disagreeing with everything you said, and getting you so confused you forgot that what you were trying to say had ever been important in the first place.

Ashley knew she could handle a doctor in a rage over a missed telephone message. She could calm an irate patient who wanted to be seen, *now*. She could manage to keep the peace in an office of twenty women with twenty very different personalities, and that wasn't easy.

But when Logan Callahan smiled, as he'd smiled at her last night, as he'd lifted that mocking eyebrow at her last night, her tongue turned into a whopping great wad of sticky bubble gum, and she couldn't get it to help her say much more than, "Fine, see you tomorrow."

She still wondered if she was angry with him for not trying to kiss her good night after walking her back to her car, or if she wanted to shake him silly for having been such a gentleman and *not* kissing her good-night.

In other words, a fairly restless night had not

helped to settle Ashley's feeling about Logan Callahan, feelings that couldn't really be called ambivalent. Ambivalence had nothing to do with one's stomach doing small flips when a man smiled at you. Not in Ashley's book, anyway.

Wrapping an oversize bath towel around her still-wet body, she tramped to her closet and looked at the half-dozen hangers and the freshly laundered white work pants draped over them. Then she turned, looked out at the rain. Nope. Not today. Not white. She wasn't *that* professional.

And that made her mad. It was one thing for her to have forgotten to put her whites in the dryer, but it was another thing for her to have to adjust her wardrobe to accommodate Logan Callahan.

She shook her head, saying, "Oh, that's good, Ashley. Now you're blaming him for asking you to stop by and look at Sandler House. You're blaming him for actually paying attention to you, listening to what you said. Maybe you can blame the rain on him, too?"

She grimaced as she stepped into jeans, zipped them. "And then, as they're carrying you off to the place with the nice padded rooms and pottery classes, you can blame him for the fact that now you're *talking* to yourself!"

The phone rang, and Ashley silently thanked it, for now she wouldn't have to talk to herself. She'd have to talk to her mom, or to Mary. Heck, for all she knew, she could be talking to both of them, considering the fact that their mom had discovered the efficiency of conference calling.

"Conference calling with Ma and sis. Oh joy. So

just *what* are you saying thanks for, Dawson?" she complained, picking up the phone and punching the Talk button. "Good morning, Ashley's House of Sin here, how may we help you?"

"You're terribly cheerful so early in the morning, sweetheart," her mother commented, reaching across the wires all the way from King of Prussia and making Ashley feel three years old again. "Or is having your mother go into immediate heart failure topping your to-do project list for the day?"

Ashley collapsed onto the side of the bed. "Hi, Mom. I thought maybe you were Mary."

"Oh, good. Frighten the child instead. That's lovely, dear. So, how was your evening?"

"Fine. We only had to call the police twice, to break up the brawl."

"Brawl? It's early, Ashley. Explain, please."

"Oh, that's right, Mom, you don't know, do you? You were only worried that I was going out on a date with someone I didn't know but who you were sure couldn't be a good person because—hey, why do you think I'd date someone who isn't a good person? I'm you're sane, levelheaded daughter, remember?"

"You are, and I'd called this morning to apologize for overreacting last night," Lindsay Dawson said, then added, "although now I may have changed my mind again."

Ashley stood up, made her way back to the closet to unearth her hiking boots, which she'd take with her in the car. "Okay, I'll explain. My date was Logan Callahan, of Callahan and Son, and he's part of the team, company, whatever that's tearing down

Sandler House next week. I went out with him, Mom,
to ask him how he could do such a thing.''

''And you fought about it?''

''No, actually, we didn't. In fact, he's even invited
me to stop by Sandler House today on my lunch
hour, to tour the place with him. I'm hoping he'll
see why the house shouldn't be torn down.''

''And what is he hoping?''

Ashley pressed her lips together, gave that a moment's thought. ''Wow, Mom, you ask good questions. I don't know what he's hoping for. No wonder
I keep you around. You're good. You're very, very
good.''

''I've had practice, sweetheart,'' Lindsay said, her
clear laughter making Ashley smile. ''Now, be a
good girl and go to work and I'll do the same. I have
a large shipment coming in this morning and have to
be at the store to unlock the door. Oh, and pay no
attention to your sister when she shows up. She was
only following orders, poor thing. Bye!''

As if on cue, the doorbell rang, and Ashley went
to answer it, letting in her sister who stepped inside,
dripping rainwater from her hot pink plastic slicker.

''Hi, Ash, got any doughnuts?'' Mary asked as she
hung her slicker on the old-fashioned wooden clothes
tree Ashley had found at a flea market and refinished.
''No? Well, I do. Fresh from the bakery. You want
jelly-filled or plain? Whoops, not fast enough, Ash.
You get the plain one.''

Ashley watched her sister head for the kitchen, and
the pot of coffee that was, thanks to the marvels of
modern technology and built-in timers, already waiting for her.

Shorter than her sister, but with the same dark brown hair and eyes, Mary hadn't taken her height from their father's side of the family the way Ashley had, and barely topped five feet, compared to Ashley's five foot six.

Mary was also, at twenty-two, two years younger than Ashley, but she was already a married woman. That was, according to their mother, because Mary had been born to grow up, marry and make some man and a gaggle of children very happy people.

Mary could sew, garden, bake like a dream. She could decorate a house, beautifully, with ten yards of material and a couple of drapery poles. She could make a room warm and inviting, her personality stamped all over it in cushions and framed photographs and some special *something* that Ashley recognized but could not really explain. Or duplicate.

In short, Mary was a Domestic Goddess, or whatever it was called. She loved being loved, she loved loving her husband, and she was, probably, the most happy person Ashley had ever met. And yet, as at home as she was *at* home, Mary had all the business acumen of their mother, which was why she ran the Allentown store, the first Lindsay's Intimates, founded by their mother.

Pouring them each cups of coffee while Ashley poured them glasses of orange juice, Mary sat herself down at the breakfast bar and patted the stool beside her. "Talk to me, sis. I've got to make a report to Mom in an hour and if you love me you won't leave me hanging out here with nothing to give her. She may be little, but she's mighty."

"She's also called you off, Mare," Ashley told

her, sliding onto the stool as she sipped at her orange juice. "As a matter of fact, she phoned a few minutes ago to apologize for butting in. You know what that means, don't you?"

Mary grimaced. "Yeah, sure do. I give you a week to either say goodbye to this Callahan guy or marry him. Otherwise, Mom's going to be up here checking him out. I don't think Paul's recovered from his Lindsay Look-over yet, and we've been married for four months."

"Several weeks and a couple of days," Ashley added, remembering their phone conversation of last night. "But seriously, Mary, it was an okay night. He listened to what I had to say, and then promised to meet with me today, over my lunch hour, to inspect Sandler House. It's probably more than I could have hoped for, considering the fact that I'd treated him pretty shabbily."

Mary set down her coffee cup, waved her jelly doughnut in Ashley's face. "No, no, no, Ash, that's not what I came here to hear. What's he *look* like? Start at the top of his head, and work your way down."

Ashley surprised herself for suddenly wishing her sister out of the apartment, out of this new, still confusing part of her life. "He's good-looking, Mare, definitely. A mop of hair that should be trimmed but actually shouldn't, if you know what I mean. Great green eyes. Tanned skin—you know, with lean cheeks with those *slashes* in them when he smiles."

She hesitated, biting her bottom lip. "He smiles a lot. Long, slow smiles that make you think of walks on the beach and long talks after midnight.'' She shook herself, quickly took a bite of doughnut.

Mary spoke around a mouthful of doughnut. "Oh, brother. Looks like Mom's radar is still working. You like him, don't you?"

Ashley took her empty orange juice glass to the sink, ran water in it. "Mary, I haven't had a date in so long I'd probably think Godzilla had a nice smile. Besides, it wasn't really a date. And neither is today. I—I think he just might be trying to *humor* me."

"Humor you? I see. And why do you suppose he would want to do that, Ashley?"

She shrugged, avoided her sister's eyes. "So that I don't handcuff myself to one of their bulldozers?" she offered, not really believing herself even as she said the words.

What she did believe was that Logan Callahan was interested in her. Which worked out fairly well, as she definitely was interested in him.

The rain stopped at eleven, and the sun was shining brightly at one o'clock as Ashley pulled her car onto the gravel construction road and parked it beside the large white trailer Logan had told her about the previous evening.

She reached over the back seat and retrieved her hiking boots, slipped off her white leather sneakers, and was just lacing up the second boot when there was a knock on the driver's side window.

Looking up, she was greeted by Logan Callahan's smile, the one that seemed such an effortless seduction. He motioned for her to unlock the door, then he opened it, leaned in to say hi. She could smell his aftershave, and if there was another man on the face of the earth who wore denim and plaid better than he did, she'd yet to meet him.

"Hi, yourself," she said, motioning for him to stand back so she could get out of the car. "You're on time. Does that mean I'm late?"

"I'll ignore that, because the sun's out, and because I'm hungry. Now, come on, we'll take the sports utility. It's too muddy for anything else and the old approach road has already been ripped out in preparation for grading the ground."

"Yes, sir, Mr. Callahan, sir," Ashley responded, mentally kicking herself for going on the attack the moment she'd opened her mouth. What was it about this man that set up all her defenses, made her seem to go out of her way to be snarky, as her mother would put it?

He helped her climb onto the high bench seat of the huge vehicle, then slammed the door on her and went around to the driver's door. "You were wrong about one thing, Ashley," he told her a few moments later, putting the vehicle in gear. "The roof is still pretty good. Slate, you know, and almost indestructible. But those broken windows sure made for a mess in the rain and snow."

"You've already looked at the house?" Ashley responded, her spirits sinking a little, as she'd hoped to give him the grand tour, tell him everything she'd learned about the history of Sandler House. Not that she'd ever seen it, been inside it. The land had been posted with No Trespassing signs even since the bed-and-breakfast had closed. That might not have been enough to stop vandals, but it had been enough to stop her and the Historical Society.

"Just a quick look through the downstairs. I saw the mantel. You're right, those have got to be bullet holes. Are you hungry? I've got a picnic basket in the back seat."

Ashley turned on the seat, saw the wicker basket behind them. "You didn't have to do that, Callahan," she told him, liking him more every minute, and not wanting to like him at all.

"It's the lunch hour, Dawson," he responded with a grin. "We both have to eat. Oh—nice boots. You'll be glad you wore them. I think about six generations of birds have been nesting in the front parlor. I swept it out, but it's not exactly hospital-sterile in there."

"You swept it out?" Really, this man was so unpredictable. She tried to picture him with a broom in his hands, and failed miserably. "Why would you do that? You're tearing the house down next week, remember?"

He put the gearshift into Park and sat back against the seat, looking at her in that way that told her he was thinking something she probably didn't want to analyze. "Is this your sales pitch, Ashley? Reminding me over and over that I'm tearing down this great architectural and historical dwelling? I may not be the world's best salesman, leaving that to my dad, but I think you might want to try for a more positive approach."

Then he reached into the back seat for the picnic basket and a large woolen blanket she hadn't noticed earlier. She didn't wait for him to come around and open her door, preferring to scramble out on her own, and leaped before she looked, landing with both feet in a deep mud puddle.

That was his fault, too!

She followed him onto the front porch of Sandler House, stamping her feet to get rid of the worst of the mud, deliberately not saying anything about the twinkle in his green eyes as he appreciated her predicament. The louse.

She looked up, indicating the porch roof, determined to begin her sales pitch without actually talking to him one-to-one again. Ever. Not in this lifetime.

"This is an add-on," she said, "and definitely not replacing any original roof." She then pointed to the doorway. "See that big fanlight over the front door? That's how the front of the house was meant to be viewed, with the door as the center of interest."

"Pretty fancy window treatment for a colonial home, don't you think?"

She nodded her agreement, still not looking at him. "The Sandlers were a wealthy family, more gentleman farmers than anything else, and they primarily resided in Philadelphia, only coming here during the summers. For the remainder of the year, John Sandler leased the place to his cousin, until that cousin was killed in one of the raids. They took his body back to Philadelphia for burial. In fact, there's only one or two Sandlers buried in local cemeteries. But the Historical Society traced them all down, and we have a fairly detailed family history on file. Shall we… um…shall we go inside?"

Logan pulled a key from his pocket and undid the large lock and chain holding the door shut. "Kind of for show, I guess, considering there's two broken windows on this floor alone, but I locked it anyway when I left this morning.''

It was cool inside, and rather dark in the hallway, thanks to the inappropriate porch roof, but Ashley's eyes became adjusted quickly and she walked down the short center hall, turning left into what had to have been the good parlor.

She couldn't believe she was finally inside Sandler House, walking among all the history to be found there, perhaps disturbing the ghosts who resided there. ''Oh, here's the mantelpiece. Isn't it gorgeous, Callahan? You could almost *stand* inside that fireplace.''

''It's solid oak,'' Logan told her, running a hand along the thick mantel that ran at least fifteen feet long above the huge stone fireplace. ''Here's the bullet holes. Only two, I'm afraid, if you were hoping for more. Someone must have dug out the bullets.''

Ashley poked a trembling finger into one of the holes, withdrew it again quickly. She didn't bother repressing the shiver than ran down her spine. ''Can you imagine what it had to be like, watching the Indians coming across the fields out there, knowing they were headed your way?''

''You saw the shutters—the ones that are left?'' Logan asked her, walking to the window. ''They closed them from the outside, then closed this second set on the inside. Here, the inside shutters are hidden in the wall, as part of the window embrasure. That was easy enough, as these walls are nearly three feet thick.''

She watched as he undid a rusty lever and opened

the bifold shutter that had been pressed flat against
the side of the window embrasure. "Wow," was all
she could say, all she could think to say. "That's a
gun slot halfway up, isn't it?"

He nodded, replacing the shutter, carefully locking
it in place. "I went downstairs to the cellars, and
there's a stone trough running through them. From
what I've read, I'd say a spring once ran right
through there, so that the residents would have water
without having to go outside. In case they couldn't
leave the house safely, you understand. Later, when
the Indian wars were over, they probably blocked off
the spring and made do with well water. The odd
thing is to remember that ancient cultures had indoor
plumbing—toilets, hot and cold running water—all
the amenities. And yet all that technology seemed to
have died out in later centuries, so that by the 1700s
homes like this one were built without indoor plumbing."

"You've done research?"

He looked at her, smiled that lazy smile. "I'm an
architect, remember? Indoor plumbing, mundane as
it is, was a very necessary part of my education."

"Well, there has to be plumbing in the house now,
as I doubt the bed-and-breakfast patrons would have
agreed to use an outhouse," Ashley said, making her
way back into the hallway, eager to do some more
exploring. More than eager to get away from Logan's
appealing presence.

She peeked into a room large enough to hold a
dining table capable of seating twenty people, then
passed through three connecting rooms whose use
escaped her. Probably sitting rooms of some sort, and

maybe the owner's private study. All the rooms were bare, with piles of dried leaves on the floor, a few spray-painted bits of graffiti on the dark oak-paneled walls. There were several empty brown bottles in one room, remnants of a party some of the vandals had carried out in the house.

Her spirits dipped with each new room she saw, until they bottomed out as she entered the huge kitchen and saw the fireplace that stood equally as large as the one in the parlor. The owners of the bed-and-breakfast had taken the modern appliances with them, but they hadn't disturbed the original dry sink or a tall wooden cabinet built into one of the walls.

She stood in he middle of the room, sighed as she considered the fireplace and sink. "It's something, I guess," she said, talking to herself, "but not that much. I hadn't realized…"

"Nothing stands still, Ashley, especially time," Logan said from behind her, and she felt his hands on her shoulders. "Now let me tell you what you aren't seeing, that I can see, okay?"

She turned around, so that he had to lift his hands, but she didn't step back, so that he also was no more than two feet away from her. Close enough to touch. Close enough to smell his aftershave, feel the power of his physical presence. Feel the traitorous urges of her own body.

"What do you see that I don't see, Callahan? I see a mess, a shell of what was once a great house. I don't know when I've been more disappointed."

He took her hand, led her back into the parlor, where the blanket and picnic basket waited. Spreading the blanket, he indicated that she should sit down while he opened one of the few remaining intact windows, letting in more of the warm, sweet-smelling spring air.

"For one, I see windows that still work, which is pretty amazing all by itself. Not replacement windows, mind you, but the originals. Nailed together with wooden pegs, the sashes fashioned out of rope—although I'm sure those ropes aren't more than twenty years old. I see the floor you're sitting on, the wide planks of solid oak also held together by wooden pegs. Dirty now, yes, and warped, but thick enough that they could be sanded, refinished. You don't get workmanship like that anymore, Ashley. The cost would be prohibitive for anyone."

She saw the soft glow in his eyes as he looked around the room, heard the admiration in his voice. Who was selling the preservation of this house to whom? She smiled, dipping her head to hide her expression. "And then there's the bannister, Callahan," she pointed out, trying to return to her role of advocate. "Is it really made of one piece of wood?"

"False advertising, I'm afraid," he told her, sitting down beside her on the blanket and opening the picnic basket. "The banister itself is one piece, and the curve in it is pretty magnificent. But the balustrades are individually carved, which only makes sense. Even wealthy Philadelphia businessmen couldn't afford what it would take to create that sort of architectural miracle. Still, the fact that it's a floating staircase, which is really rare, more than makes up for the lapse. You like fried chicken?"

She laughed out loud as he pulled and a red-and-white cardboard container out of the picnic basket and placed it on the blanket. "And here I thought you stayed up all night, cooking for us. But the basket is a nice touch, I have to admit."

They spoke of other things as they ate their lunch. Silly things, serious things, touching on subjects she'd forget in an hour, those she'd remember all of her life, even after Logan Callahan was nothing more than a distant memory.

Mostly, she'd remember how he looked, sitting cross-legged on the blanket, munching on a chicken leg, using the bone for emphasis as he stabbed the air while making a point about floor joists and how, yeah, they were sort of necessary if you didn't want the house to fall down.

They discussed her family—how he'd gotten her to speak of her mother and sister she didn't know, but he had a way of asking without prying, and she spent a good ten minutes telling him about Mary and her mom.

She told him how her widowed mother had been left with two young girls to raise and had boldly taken the small amount of money they'd had and built a successful women's lingerie store in Allentown. She told him about her mother's new store, in King of Prussia, the thriving mail-order business her mother had begun once she'd discovered the joys of the Internet.

Her pride in her mother was probably obvious to him, but Ashley didn't care. She'd be happy if she became half the woman her mother was, with half her courage and love of life.

She told him how she'd worked in the Allentown store as a teenager, very much against her wishes, and somehow admitted to the fact that she'd been a lot happier in jeans than in lace, a lot more satisfied nursing sick animals as a volunteer at the local shelter.

Her mother still commandeered her at times, using one of her famous Lindsay Guilt Trips in talking her into helping at the store during the busy Valentine's, Mother's Day and Christmas selling seasons, but Ashley also admitted that her mother had seen very early on that, while Mary loved the business, her oldest daughter's interests lay elsewhere.

It wasn't until she had finished telling him about her Specialized Business, Secretarial Science and Medical Administrative Assistant Associate's degree that she realized that, one, she'd been doing most of the talking and that, two, her lunch hour was almost over and they hadn't even toured the upstairs of Sandler House.

And that, three, she still didn't know much of anything about Logan Callahan.

Mumbling something about the time, she began picking up the remains of their meal, stuffing it all back into the box, placing the box back into the basket. "Not that another bit of garbage lying about would really mean anything, I suppose, but we really shouldn't leave this," she said, knowing she was beginning to babble.

He knew it, too, damn him. She could tell by the amusement in his eyes, the way he watched her as she fluttered and fussed.

"So, what are you going to do about the house?" she asked at last, as he helped her to her feet, picked up the blanket and folded it over his arm.

"What do you want me to do about the house, Ashley?" he countered as they walked to the door, out onto the porch.

She looked back at him, trying to read his expression, and tripped over a loose board, her arms flying out at her sides as she tried to keep her balance.

He caught her of course, just like all the best heroes do, and the next thing she knew she was pressed against him, chest to chest, looking up into those maddening green eyes.

His lips were warm as they touched against hers, lightly, not at all threateningly. Almost politely.

She closed her eyes, feeling his arms sliding around her back, feeling herself melt against him.

He kissed as he did everything else. Slowly, almost lazily. Taking his time about fitting his mouth against hers, taking his time in deepening the kiss, taking his time as he waited for her to slide her arms around his waist, hang on to him as the world exploded behind her eyes in every color of the rainbow.

And then he was holding her hand, leading her across the muddy ground, back to the sports-utility vehicle.

He didn't say anything, and she couldn't trust herself to say anything, until she was in her own car once more, nervously fumbling to insert the key in the ignition.

"Dinner tonight?" he asked her in that husky voice that held the power to make her toes numb, holding open the door when she tried to close it.

She agreed, somehow, which was no mean feat when she considered that her tongue had turned to a

wad of sticky bubble gum again, and drove away
knowing she'd see him again in a few hours.

She smiled, feeling pretty good about herself,
about her very interesting lunch hour, until she realized he hadn't answered her question. She still
didn't know what he was going to do about Sandler
House.

What a maddening man!

Chapter Four

Logan wondered if maybe he had a fever, was, as his grandmother used to say, "sickening for something." What else could explain why he'd used up fifteen minutes, and some choice swear words, tying a maroon-and-blue striped tie around his neck with what amounted to one-and-a-half hands.

Why had he bothered with a suit at all? Who was he out to impress?

Well, those questions both had the same pretty simple answer...

As he drove his freshly washed Mercedes through the well-designed apartment complex, looking for Ashley's building, he reviewed in his mind all that had happened since she'd shown up at the site earlier.

He'd been surprised at how happy he'd been to see her compact car pull onto the construction road, then realized he'd half believed she wouldn't show up. Not after the way he'd teased her the night before, the way they had struck such sparks off each other.

He liked the sparks, personally. She kept him on his toes, and bantering with her—did people still say "bantering"?—had been a lot of fun. But that didn't mean she'd enjoyed it, or him, and she just as easily could have thought him to be more than a little bit of a smart-ass.

So he'd seen her car, cut himself off in the middle of a sentence as he'd been speaking with the site manager, and come out of the trailer bound and determined to be a real nice guy. A likable guy. A guy determined to be good.

Then she'd made that crack about him being on time, so that she, in turn, must be late, and they were off, picking up where they'd ended the previous evening.

And, damn, but he'd enjoyed himself!

He'd liked watching her walk around Sandler House, reverently touching her hand to doorjambs, sighing as she saw the damage inside the old building. He'd felt so sorry for her as she slowly realized that maybe, just maybe, her wish was more of a hopeful dream, and that the house was beyond repair.

That was probably for the best. If he wanted to keep to the job schedule, there wasn't room for more than bulldozing down the building Monday morning and moving in earnest on the next step: grading the land where the new building would rise over the course of the following months.

Of course, that's how he'd thought before he'd kissed her, before she'd kissed him back.

That's when his mind had begun to muddle.

He was twenty-seven years old. He'd kissed before, been kissed before. Been a lot more than kissed, damn it.

But he'd never kissed Ashley Dawson before, and he suddenly knew, somewhere deep inside him, that the time for variety was over. This woman, this prickly, funny, determined woman was the woman he wanted to kiss, to hold, to love, for the rest of his life.

That's probably why he'd worn the suit, had the car washed. It was too already way too late to make a good first impression, even a good second impression, but tonight could be the beginning of their real courtship. Courtship? Bantering? Man, he was in real trouble, and sounding more like his dad than felt comfortable.

Especially since his dad, the great Ryan Callahan, had drummed it into his son's head all his twenty-seven years that impulsive actions almost always ended in disaster.

Good thing the old man was in Tokyo…because, if their kiss had affected Ashley as much as it had affected him, Logan had some pretty impulsive actions in mind.

He was half-leaning on the doorjamb, one hand raised against the wood as he propped himself up, the other, uninjured hand holding a bouquet of plump yellow roses, when Ashley opened the door.

"Hi," he said, smiling at her. "Only twenty minutes late. I think that's a new record. But the first shop didn't have yellow roses. I don't know why, but I think you were born to be given yellow roses."

"Callahan?" she pretty much squeaked back at him, looking him up and down in a darn good imitation of stunned disbelief. "What in the world happened to you? And don't tell me you went to all this effort just to go out to dinner to me. You were probably at the mall, and somehow fell into a clothing store, and into that suit."

She narrowed her eyes, looked at him even more closely. "Who tied your tie?"

His grin spread. "'I've always been able to depend on the kindness of strangers,'" he semiquoted from the old movie he'd seen on television last night in his hotel room.

She let go of the doorknob and stood back, allowing him to enter. "With anyone else, I'd say that's only a hopeful wish. You, Callahan, I believe. I'm willing to bet little old ladies see you passing by and rush out of their houses to offer you plates of fresh-baked cookies, then ask if they can do your laundry for you."

"It's sort of frightening to remember we only met yesterday, Ashley," he told her, handing her the bouquet and watching her walk toward the kitchen half-hidden behind a dividing wall. "You seem able to see through me like the proverbial pane of glass. I'm trying to decide whether or not that's a good thing."

She paused as she entered the kitchen, looked back at him—only her head and shoulders visible from behind the wall. "That would depend, Callahan. A good thing for you, or for *me?*" Then she grinned, and disappeared.

He wanted to follow her, like a puppy who'd had one treat and hungered for another.

Instead, he stayed where he was and inspected the living room, seeing Ashley's personality stamped all over it.

She liked plants, lots of plants. In fact, as the curtains were open on either side of the French doors, he could see about two dozen terracotta pots sitting on the small balcony, all of them full of flowers. Except for the ones holding what he felt sure were tomato plants and pepper plants.

This was a woman who should have a huge garden to play in, a woman who liked burying her fingers into the soil, bringing that soil to life.

The furnishings in the living room were definitely eclectic, ranging from the massive, cushiony sofa and love seat done in classic white—probably with down pillows for comfort. She sure had a thing for pillows, because there were at least a dozen of them scattered across the couches, all of them done in dark paisley or green-and-blue stripes.

He could make love to her on one of those couches, the two of them swallowed up in the comfort of them, cocooned by down as they leisurely explored each other, learned each other. Oh yeah. Definitely.

He shook himself back to attention, and to sanity, and continued his inventory.

Lots of glass, lots of brass, and yet there was an antique coat rack in one corner, a lovely old, cherry wood curio cabinet in another. White Berber at his feet, a few small, darkly patterned Oriental carpets scattered over it. One dark blue barrel chair, a good-sized television set, a pretty nice stereo tuned to a country rock station.

The dark blue walls were hung with faces, lots of
faces, as if she'd welcomed permanent company into
her home. He recognized Rembrandt's portrait of
himself as a young man, an El Greco—Storm Over
Toledo, he believed—and several more prints of old
masters that somehow all looked so right in this
room. She'd lit the pictures with brass lamps that
hung over them, and brass sconces and a few out-
croppings of pedestal, each holding a small vase, or
little boxes, even a couple with plants sitting on
them.

Not cluttered, just full. Ashley liked her life *full*.

A huge landscape, probably of rural Rome, held
pride of place over the longer couch, and Logan wondered if Rome were a dream to her, or if the picture
was there to keep her memory of a visit to Italy alive.

He admired her bold choice of colors, her interest
in art, the whimsy of the brass cat standing on the
floor beside the blue chair.

"I didn't have any vases the right size," Ashley
said as she returned to the room, carrying the roses
that now rested inside a big, round, dark blue enamel
coffeepot. "Hope these lovely flowers don't mind the
hopelessly homespun look," she ended, placing the
pot in the middle of the glass-topped brass coffee
table, then standing back, grimacing. "Mary would
have done it so much better. Of course, she got a
half-dozen crystal vases—and three toaster ovens—
for wedding presents."

Personally, Logan couldn't see how anyone could
do it better, and said so, adding, "I think you've
done a great job in this whole room. But I guess even

that compliment doesn't get me the cook's tour of the rest of the apartment?''

She straightened, having bent to adjust one of the blooms, and grinned at him. "Since my breakfast dishes are still soaking in the sink, and the only other rooms are my bedroom and bath, I'd say you got that in one, cowboy," she quipped easily, smoothing down the skirt of her simple black dress—the short, sleeveless creation that showed her both her bare arms and long, straight legs to advantage. Logan's advantage.

"You look wonderful, you know," he said, thinking he'd probably never uttered such a lame compliment in his life.

Ashley pushed a chin-length lock of hair behind her ear and looked at him levelly. Well, almost levelly—even in her three-inch black heels, she rose only to a most comfortable chin level with him. "Thank you, Callahan. And, all joking aside, I think you clean up pretty good yourself. Shall we go? I told you I'd make reservations for seven, but I really made them for seven-thirty, so if we leave now we'll actually be on time."

He laughed out loud, opened the door, swept her a pretty good imitation of a courtly bow, then patted her on the behind as she walked through the doorway ahead of her.

She looked back at him, laughed, and Logan relaxed for the first time since he'd kissed her that afternoon...and began looking forward to kissing her again.

He liked watching her eat. Her movements were graceful, her table manners exquisite, but she couldn't hide her very real enjoyment of good food. Her first bite of shrimp cocktail had her closing her eyes in ecstasy, and if that denuded lobster shell was any indication, she'd heartily approved of the main course.

He'd dated so many women who picked at house salads without dressing and mostly drank their dinners—bottled water, that is. But not Ashley. Her hectic life-style probably accounted for the fact that her body showed no sign of overindulgence, and not some idiotic, purposeful semistarvation.

Everything about her showed her great love of life, and her willingness to embrace it with both hands. Her choice of career, her interest in the world around her, the vibrant colors in her home, the way she enjoyed her food.

She was a passionate woman, a woman capable of great passion. He knew that from the way she'd responded to his kiss. But he didn't believe she was indiscriminately passionate.

No, he might have sensed her passion, but he'd also sensed her initial shock, her momentary confusion. He'd felt the tenseness of her posture as she tried to come to grips with her own reaction to their kiss, the slow relaxation of her body as she finally gave in to that passionate side of herself.

She was probably still trying, five short hours later, to understand *why* she had reacted as she had, and she probably was more than a little angry with him for kissing her, for confusing her.

After all, she'd met him, been prepared to despise him as some Philistine out to pave over America with a bunch of ugly glass buildings and one big parking lot. The fact that she had melted into his arms not twenty-four hours later probably had her caught between being disgusted with herself and wanting to string him up by his thumbs.

Almost as if she'd read his mind, she folded her linen napkin, placed it beside her plate, propped her elbows on the table and her chin in her hands, looking very much like a woman about to do battle.

"Okay, Callahan. We've wined. We've dined. We've talked about the Phillies—and your hope that they'll win the pennant this year."

"We've put several men on the moon, Ashley," he countered, playing for time. "It could happen."

"Don't interrupt, please. We've discussed world peace and we're both for it, definitely. I know how you broke your arm when you were twelve, and you know I got straight A's in Biology and flunked Spanish. Twice. Don't you think it's time we got around to why we're really here?"

Logan folded his own napkin, taking his time about the thing, propped his own elbows on the table, his own chin in his hands, and grinned across the table. "I'm here because I want to kiss you again, Ashley. I've been thinking about it all day. That, and how much I enjoy watching you try to hold on to your temper. Like now. And you're pretty mad at me right now, aren't you?"

She dropped her arms, sat back against the seat with a small thud. "You're impossible, Callahan, and I think you know it," she gritted out, frowning at him. And then she smiled, probably not even realizing that she'd raised one finger to her lips, as if reliving their kiss. "It *was* pretty good, though, wasn't it?"

"Good? Is that all you can say? Good? And here I thought you had a pretty good grasp of vocabulary. I'd call it fantastic. Mind-blowing, eye-opening, and pretty damn scary. Or am I overreacting?"

She adjusted her posture, becoming more defensive than aggressive. She lowered her eyes, began fiddling with the handle of her fork. "No, Callahan, I don't think you are." Then she lifted her eyes, and her chin, and added, "Which doesn't mean I like you. Just that I...that I...well, that I don't *hate* you anymore."

"That's a step up, I suppose," Logan said, nodding to the waiter, who brought them the dessert menu, which they both waved away, and then cleared away the dishes. Once the man was gone, he added, "But you'll hate me again when I tear down Sandler House on Monday, right?"

She turned the fork over, turned it over again. "I don't know," she said, so quietly Logan had to lean forward to hear her. "It *is* pretty much of a mess, isn't it? The Historical Society certainly doesn't have enough money to restore it to its former beauty, and the government turned us down when we asked for a grant. Not historic enough a building, you understand. I kept researching, hoping Washington had slept there or something, but with no luck. Nobody exactly got all excited when we held a few bake sales and other fund-raisers last summer, before the land was sold to the company you're building the factory for...excuse me. The telecommunications center."

"You know why we're building it where we are,

don't you, Ashley?'' he asked her. "The Sandlers had the right idea, putting the house where they put it. The location is perfect, really the only logical place on the whole forty acres where the building could be shown to its best advantage.''

He resettled himself in his chair, sinking his teeth into his subject. "The slight rise lends itself to some really innovative architecture, which is rare in this age of great big square or rectangular buildings that just sort of *sit* there, surrounded by parking lots. Working with the different gradings, I was able to have our team draw up a truly interesting plan, one with different levels, some pretty novel uses of space. On the west side, the side with the largest drop-off, we've actually been able to incorporate below-ground delivery docks, so that the tractor-trailers won't even be seen. Red brick, lots of white wood, honest-to-God peaked roofs instead of a big, ugly box with a flat lid. Modern, yet classic; easy on the eyes, yet fully functional...I'm getting carried away, aren't I?'' he asked, his look apologetic.

"No, no you're not. It sounds lovely, Callahan. Really. I just don't know how you can be so enthused about creating something beautiful if it means destroying something beautiful. Or at least it once was beautiful.''

Was this the time to tell her Sandler House hadn't appeared on any of the site drawings he'd seen, any of the descriptions he'd read before turning the nuts and bolts of the project over to his staff of architects?

Probably not. It would sound too self-serving. Besides, he was still more than moderately angry that the house *hadn't* been there, and felt like a fool for not having come to physically inspect the site for himself before now, not checking up on his subordinates. Maybe he *was* getting lazy, which was no excuse. None.

Instead he said, "I ran some figures this afternoon, taking the local contractor along with me as we toured the house together. I don't think you want to hear them, Ashley, because they're pretty high. Not that it matters, because the plans are drawn, the workers have been hired, and the budget most definitely established. I can't see my clients springing for a whole new set of plans and a huge delay in beginning the construction, can you?"

She shrugged her shoulders, sighed. "No. No, I can't. And it is their property. They bought it. I guess they can do what they want with it."

Logan laughed. "So speaks the woman who has never had to deal with local zoning boards. Ashley, it took over a year to get these plans approved. So it's not just the money, or putting the building on a less desirable portion of the land. It's time, Ashley. And time *is* money."

"So there's nothing we can do—nothing I can do, I mean," she said, correcting herself, as if remembering that, yes, Logan Callahan was still the enemy. "Well, I guess that's that. Do you think we could go back once more? I'd really like to see the upstairs, take some photographs before Sandler House becomes a mass of rubble."

"Yeah," he said, feeling like the lowest of worms, "we can do that."

He pulled away from her, only slightly, looking down at her in the light cast by the brass lamp tacked to the brick wall of her apartment building. "Even better than the first one," he told her, lowering his head once more, this time pushing back her hair, pressing his lips against the soft flesh of her throat. "And she tastes good, too."

They had finished their meal an hour ago, and spent the intervening time driving around the city, Ashley pointing out sites of historic interest.

The old stone church on Hamilton Street that housed a replica of the Liberty Bell because the original had been brought to the city during the Revolutionary War, to be hidden in the church basement.

The soldiers and sailors monument in the city square. The old courthouse, a stone house the Historical Society *had* been able to rescue and bring back to its former glory.

She had such pride in her voice as she told him of the rather extensive library the Historical Society had gathered for public use, of the entire downtown neighborhoods that were slowly being reclaimed and returned to the glory of the years the houses were built, most of them predating the Civil War.

And then, while sharing Italian ices at a walk-up storefront, she'd laughed and confessed why she'd joined the Historical Society in the first place. "It was a man, of course," she'd told him. "My mother dragged me to some small lecture, thinking I needed more outside activity now that I was working so hard at the Medical Center, and he was the speaker. Mom thought I had gotten caught up in the speech, while I knew I had gotten caught up in wire-rimmed glasses, a small, shaggy beard, and a tweed jacket with those suede elbows, you know? Well, the bloom went off that rose in a single date, as he seemed to delight in talking about two things—himself, and himself—but by then it was too late. I was hooked on the Society, and have been pretty active in the group ever since. I guess I'm just a sucker for defenseless things in need of help. Injured animals, sick people, old, unloved buildings."

She couldn't know it, but Logan had felt himself falling more and more in love with her with every word she said. In fact, although it blew his mind how much he wanted her physically, the real surprise was in how much he just wanted to *be* with her, talk with her, enjoy her company. Love was great, but *liking* her? Liking her just felt *good.*

Now he breathed in her perfume, a simple one reminding him of spring rain, and amused himself by nuzzling her neck as she rubbed her hands up and down his back.

"I imagine old Mrs. Blocker has her binoculars out, enjoying the heck out of this," Ashley said at last, her voice rather muffled against his shoulder. "But that doesn't mean I want you to stop, Callahan, in case you're wondering."

He took hold of her shoulders, held her away from him, looked down into her eyes; those laughing, smoldering brown eyes. "Does it mean you're inviting me in?" he asked, already knowing the answer. It was too soon, probably too soon for both of them. But, damn it, he wanted her so badly.

She went up on tiptoe, kissed his mouth. "Nope. I'm not that strong, Callahan."

He turned his head, looked across the courtyard,

saw the curtains drawn back in the front window of
6A. "In that case, hold onto your garters, Mrs.
Blocker, because I'm going to kiss her again," Logan said, then followed his joking threat with action.

Logan was on Ashley's doorstep again the following morning, a heavy bag of Danishes and bagels in
his hand. She'd invited him in.

He'd driven her to work, picked her up for lunch,
taken her out to dinner.

The routine continued for the remainder of Ashley's work week. Fantastic, glorious days, although
Logan never quite got himself back into Ashley's
apartment after dinner, and they both knew why.

Mrs. Blocker had pretty much taken up permanent
residence in front of her window, and she probably
knew why, too.

The electricity between Logan and Ashley was po-
tent, hot, and tossing sparks everywhere. Their union
was inevitable, but even without saying a word to
each other on the subject, both seemed to know that
the moment had to be right, the timing perfect. Because when they did make love it would mean that
they'd never let each other go. Never.

In a perfect world, Logan believed, he and Ashley
would have continued with their relationship, slowly
deepening it, and most probably coming to the con-
clusion already firmly planted in his mind—that of
wedding her, bedding her, and the two of them living
happily ever after.

But, as Logan also knew, the world is far from
perfect.

Saturday morning, as room service delivered his

breakfast and a complimentary copy of the local
newspaper, and as he sat munching on wheat toast
and reading the Local section, the bottom fell out of
all of his fantasies.

"Fight Looms At Construction Site," the headline
read, the story above the fold on the first page of the
Local section, the smaller headline carrying the tale.
"'The time has come to draw the line against wanton
destruction of valuable historical sites, and Sandler
House is where we draw it,' says Carl Whittier,
newly resigned Historical Society spokesperson."

Logan looked at the picture accompanying the article. Gold-rimmed glasses. Shaggy beard. A glimpse
of tweed jacket.

"Damn."

Logan read the article quickly, his breakfast forgotten. It seemed that good old Suede Elbows had
resigned his post at the Historical Society in protest
and gathered himself a more radical splinter group
intent on making sure no bulldozers came within fifty
yards of Sandler House the following Monday morning.

Had Ashley known about this all week, and not
said anything? Was her mention of Suede Elbows the
other night just random conversation, or her way of
warning him? And, if she knew about Whittier's
plans, was she also a part of this splinter group?

Would she answer the phone if he called her, now,
at eight in the morning? Would she still want to take
that drive to the New Jersey shore they'd talked
about, want to walk with him on the beach?

Or would he go out to the site this morning to see
her walking up and down in front of the construction

road, carrying a placard calling Callahan and Son and their client nasty names?

He didn't want to call her. He didn't want to know. He reached for the phone....

Chapter Five

"Yes, Mary, I saw the paper," Ashley said, pacing her bedroom, wishing her sister off the phone, wishing her sister here in her apartment, to comfort her. "Yes, I know they start picketing today. No, I don't know if Callahan knows."

She heard a beep on the phone, indicating that another call was coming in, and grimaced. "I think he's on the other line, Mare," she said, her stomach filled with fluttering butterflies. "I can't talk to him yet. I just can't. I have to get my head on straight first."

While her sister very reasonably pointed out that open and honest communication is the most important thing two people can share, Ashley picked up the local section of the newspaper and stuck her tongue out at Carl Whittier.

"I'm sure you're right, Mary," she interrupted as her sister was beginning to sound like a Sunday sermon. "But it isn't that easy. I *know* these people. Their intentions are honorable, even if their tactics leave a lot to be desired. I feel…well, I feel like I've been asked to choose sides."

She listened for another few moments, shaking her head. "No, Mare, not like the guy in *Les Misérables*. What? Yes, his name was Marius. But he was choosing between his love for Cosette and a doomed revolution, a truly hopeless cause…yes, okay, all right, maybe I *do* see the parallels. But what am I supposed to do, Mary? These are my friends. How do I abandon them?"

She closed her eyes, picturing her friends carrying placards, possibly trespassing onto private property, maybe even doing just as Callahan had suggested— chaining or handcuffing themselves to bulldozers.

Then she pictured the police on the scene; limp, uncooperative bodies being dragged off to jail like modern-day martyrs; and news reporters and photographers crawling all over the place like grinning vultures.

And Callahan in the middle of it, wearing his lazy smile, pushing a hand through his shaggy hair, explaining that time was money.

They'd hate him…except for the old ladies who'd come out to the site, bringing him home-baked cookies.…

"What? I'm sorry, Mary, I wasn't listening," she admitted as her sister repeated her name across the phone line. She listened for a moment, then nodded her head. "Okay. Right. I'll call him at the hotel, explain that I didn't know this was going to happen—and I didn't, damn it!—then beg him not to call the police on Carl and the others until I have a chance to talk some sense into them. If you let me get off the phone any time soon, that is, Mare.''

Thanking her sister again, her sister who first had to remind her that Ashley had phoned *her*, and not the other way around, Ashley pushed the Disconnect button, then stared at the portable phone for long moments before tossing it onto the bed and heading for the shower.

Her phone call to Callahan could wait. Wait until she was sure he was awake. Until he'd read the newspaper, if he even had it. Wait until his first anger blew itself out.

Wait until she could gather her courage together and hope to say anything even mildly coherent.

She was just blow-drying her hair when the doorbell rang and she froze in the act of curving a lock of hair over her brush and stared, bug-eyed, at her reflection in the mirror.

"Could be the landlord, checking on the plumbing," she told herself. "Boy Scouts collecting cans for recycling. The paper boy wanting to be paid. My fairy godmother come to rescue me from all this."

Or it could be Callahan.

Probably was Callahan.

"Just a minute, please," she called out loudly, turning off the hair dryer and grabbing a tube of lipstick, knowing makeup to be a flimsy armor, but right now she'd take anything she could get.

It was Callahan.

"You didn't answer your phone," he said, brushing past her and walking into the living room without being invited, without kissing her good morning, "so I thought I'd come by and see if I could help you ink placards."

"Ink plac—oh, isn't *that* nice! Do I get a last request, or are you just here to hang me without a trial and have done with it?" she muttered, following him to the kitchen, where he was already pouring himself a cup of coffee. For a man who barely ever looked like he was moving, he sure could move fast. Right now he was obviously very rapidly leaping toward conclusions.

He leaned back against the edge of the counter, the cup of black coffee in his hand, half-lifted to his lips. He inventoried her clothing, from her Allentown Business School sweatshirt, to her jeans, to her hiking boots. That irritating, fascinating left eyebrow was raised in speculation. "So I'm wrong? You're not heading out to the site?"

"Yes, I am going out there, but—"

"Well, isn't that just *great!* Just Jim-by-damn-*dandy!*" Logan slammed the coffee cup down with a bang, sloshing hot coffee onto his hand.

She reacted quickly as he swore under his breath, grabbing his arm and leading him to the sink, running cold water over his hand. "I'm not going out there to march with them, Callahan," she told him, too angry to measure her words. "I'm just going out there to protect them from you."

"Protect them from—what do you think *I'm* going to do, Ashley? Have them all clapped in irons? Hell, they probably already are—trespassing on the property, chained together and holding hands as they circle Sandler House. I've seen this before, you know."

That stopped her. "You've seen this before? You've *done* this before? Torn down old buildings, that is." She turned off the water, threw him a dish towel to dry his hand. "How many times, Callahan? Callahan and Son is a big Philadelphia company. You probably do this every day, don't you? Knock down old homes, destroy history, all in the name of profit. Boy oh boy, you think you know somebody, think you lo…"

Her voice trailed off as she looked at him, her cheeks suddenly gone hot as he returned her look, saying nothing, revealing nothing.

"Well, are you going to answer me? Are you going to say *anything?* Damn it, Callahan, don't you have *anything* to say to me?"

He stepped close to her, tipped up her chin with one long finger, kissed her rather thoroughly. A kiss of admission? A goodbye kiss? She didn't know, didn't want to know.

"I've got to go, make sure everything I've ordered is in place. I'll see you out at the site," he said finally, handing her the dish towel, then walking out of her apartment.

Out of her life?

Everything I've ordered.

Those words kept repeating themselves in Ashley's brain and she tried to interpret them, make some sense of them.

What would he have ordered done at the site on a Saturday?

They'd planned a drive to New Jersey, not coming back to town until late tonight.

Tomorrow they were to drive out to Sandler House one last time, so that she could tour the old homestead, take dozens of pictures for the Historical Society. Touch the handrail of that magnificent staircase, press her hands against the cool grey stone of the fireplaces.

Say goodbye.

Then, Monday morning, the bulldozers would move in, and Sandler House would be reduced to a pile of stones and wood, gone forever from the landscape.

So what had he planned to "order" done on the Saturday before the demolition? His words didn't make sense, when seen in the context of his job.

That left only last-minute orders, probably issued right after he'd seen the morning paper. Guards. Police. Warrants. Her friends being met by the law, then carted off to jail as trespassers.

Is that what he'd meant? Having torn down old buildings before, by his own admission, had he had enough practice in circumventing concerned citizens who protested such destruction? Did Callahan and Son have this sort of procedure down pat, perfected over time? Was there a Callahan and Son Corporate Plan of Action Memo already prepared for such instances?

Ashley picked up her car keys, knowing she had been stalling, not wanting to get in her car, drive out to the site, watch as Callahan ordered her friends arrested.

She didn't want to watch the man she loved—yes, loved—in his role of big businessman. She liked him much better on the dance floor, or feeding the ducks at Trexler Park, or holding her hand, stroking his thumb along her palm, as they sat in a dark movie theater.

They'd packed so much into this week, and yet still knew so little about each other. Because she could have sworn he wasn't the sort to cold-bloodedly have people carted off to jail for their beliefs.

And how little did he know her, to think that she'd actually chain herself to a bulldozer, condone such an obviously illegal action?

I was voted down.

"Oh, brother," she said, grimacing as the memory of her attempt at wry humor came back to slap her square in her credibility. She'd only been joking when she said it was her idea to chain them all to the bulldozers.

But that had been early in their relationship, and he probably remembered her words, and more probably had believed them. No wonder his green eyes had flashed ice at her this morning, no wonder he hadn't been all that surprised to see her dressed in jeans and hiking boots instead of a flowing spring dress perfect for a long walk on a New Jersey beach.

He thought she was a *radical!*

So? She thought he was a corporate monster with a bottom line for a heart.

Wow, now there was a basis for a lifelong love....

The area of Hamilton Boulevard where the new telecommunications center was to be built was also the home of several other huge corporations and a considerable scattering of shopping malls, fast-food restaurants and supermarkets. Even though the industrial plants were, for the most part, empty over the weekends, the traffic on the street was considerable, nearly as bad as on the weekdays. It took Ashley over a half hour to crawl down the Boulevard to the site.

Once there, she could understand more of the problem. Everyone who'd gone out to work, or to shop, or to eat, had to pass by the site, and it seemed nobody wanted to pass by without rubbernecking toward the crowd of people chanting and holding up signs as they trespassed on the construction road.

There were already two patrol cars with flashing lights parked on the side of the road, already two policemen standing in the center lane of the road, directing traffic, urging motorists to keep moving, keep moving.

In short, Carl Whittier and his pals—her friends—had created a real mess.

And it was bound to get worse.

Ashley slowed down—not much, as traffic was already at a crawl—and put on her turn signal, hoping the policeman would let her make a left onto the property. He looked at her as if she'd just landed from Mars, shook his head, and waved her off.

In the end, she'd parked at the shopping mall down the street and walked back toward the site, which gave her plenty of time to watch, to listen, to cringe as she wished everybody would go home and stop making such idiots out of themselves.

Carl Whittier had a bullhorn, and for a usually shy man, he didn't seem to have any trouble yelling into it, extolling passersby to stop their cars, get out, join the protest.

More than a few of them did.

Still, it didn't make for much of a crowd, not more than forty or fifty people. Hardly the makings of a mob, or a riot.

But, then, it was only ten o'clock. There was still plenty of time for both.

As she got closer she saw Maryjane Hastings, Bonnie Kauffman, George O'Neill, and at least five more faces she recognized from the Historical Society.

Maryjane Hastings she could understand, as the town librarian had had a major crush on Carl for at least a decade, not that the man had ever noticed her.

Bonnie was Maryjane's friend, which explained her presence, if not her pith helmet. George O'Neill was eighty-five, and probably figured this might be his last time to try a little civil disobedience on for size.

As for the others, they all looked pretty bewildered by all the cars, people and noise—Carl was still bellowing—and more than a few also looked as if they were in search of a graceful exit.

A woman in a flowered shirtwaist brushed past Ashley, turning back to tell her husband to hurry, so they could get it all on videotape, maybe sell the tape to the local television stations.

Personally, Ashley thought they'd probably have a better shot peddling the tape to one of those TV shows showcasing funny home videos.

Somebody was selling supermarket brand sodas out of the back of his pickup truck, doing a brisk business.

A few hard-hatted construction workers were mill-ing around about thirty feet from the sign-waving protesters, one of them calling Carl names that probably had a lot to do with his plaid Bermuda shorts and black shoes and socks.

All that was needed were three rings and a couple of lion tamers, and they'd have a real circus.

The only thing—person—missing was Logan Callahan.

"Carl," Ashley said, elbowing her way through the thin crowd, trying to get Whittier's attention. "Carl, what in hell do you think you're going to accomplish with this?"

Carl looked at her, said, "Ashley, I knew you'd come!" then winced, switched off the bullhorn that had just broadcast his comment to everyone. "I'm sorry. I keep doing that. I haven't acquired much experience with such implements, you know, but needs must when the Devil drives. I think it's going quite well, don't you? Oh, it's early days, but by Monday we should be a real force."

"Sure. Right," Ashley responded, wondering how ardent Carl's supporters would be if Monday turned out to be a rainy spring day. "But Carl, I have to tell you, I think you're beating a dead horse here."

He ignored her. The man, for all his meek, rather nerdy appearance—she had long ago adjusted her description of him from scholarly to just nerdy—had an extremely high opinion of the rightness of any plan that happened to pop into his mind. It was clear that he thought he'd found a winner in this public protest, and Ashley doubted anything she said could save him from an ignominious exist via the paddy wagon.

"I can't believe you resigned from the Historical Society," she said, hoping she could keep him from turning the bullhorn back on, agitating the crowd any further. "And the others? Did you all resign?"

Whittier pulled himself up to his full height, squared his shoulders. "There comes a time, Ashley, when a man has to stand up for what he believes. Sandler House must not be destroyed."

"You haven't seen it, but I have. It already *is* destroyed, Carl," Ashley told him, tugging on his arm as he turned on the bullhorn, began addressing the crowd.

"Attention everyone, please. I'm happy to announce that the Historical Society's correspondence secretary is here with us today, standing in solidarity with us. As one of the staunchest supporters of the unfortunately defunct Save Sandler House Committee, she's quite knowledgeable on the history of this grand old homestead. Ashley, please tell us all a little about Sandler House."

He pushed the bullhorn at her. She pushed it back.

"Ah, she needs a little encouragement, ladies and gentlemen," Carl said, sounding like a really bad emcee at an amateur talent contest. If he said, "Let's put our hands together for the little lady," she was going to flatten him, right where he stood.

The crowd clapped, some of them enthusiastically, some because, hey, what they heck, they were there, why not enjoy themselves? The construction workers began a chant, something that sounded a lot like, "Jobs first, America first." It didn't seem to fit the moment, but they did seem to be having a good time shaking their fists and shouting.

Ashley had been wrong. They didn't need the three rings, or the lion tamers. The circus was already most definitely in town.

Not able to see a way for a graceful exit, Ashley finally took the bullhorn, held it up to her mouth. "Clear the area now and nobody gets hurt," was the thought that came to her mind, but when she opened her mouth what came out was, "Sandler House was built in the middle 1750s, although no one knows the exact date. The reasons for this are many. One is that records were not kept quite as well as we could hope, and the fact that, during the Great Depression, many homeowners were convinced to sell the dated stones most houses had under the peak of the roof on one side of the house. Collectors looking for historical artifacts went around the country collecting these stones and people without much money were more than happy to sell them. That's why, as you drive through the area and see old fieldstone farmhouses, you'll also often see cement patching on one side of the house, up under the peak of the roof."

"History for sale, ladies and gentlemen," Whittier bellowed, pulling the bullhorn away from Ashley for a moment. "For sale, for destruction. But no more! The bulldozers, ladies and gentlemen, stop here. No more, no more, *no more!*"

After doing his quick rendition of a rabble-rouser he smiled almost shyly at Ashley, patted her arm, handed the bullhorn back to her. "Gee, thanks a heap, Carl," she said, quickly turning her head as a photographer wearing a ball cap with the name of the local newspaper on it raised his camera in her direction.

That's when she saw Callahan, standing on the edge of the crowd, his arms folded over his chest, a slow smile on his face, his eyes shadowed beneath his Phillies cap, which didn't mean she didn't know they were smiling, too. He lifted one hand, lazily waved at her, blew a kiss in her direction.

Obviously he saw her predicament, sensed her unwillingness to be seen as a part of this useless protest. Just as obviously he had forgiven her, not that he shouldn't be on his knees for ever having doubted her in the first place.

She returned his smile, deciding that he should be punished, just a little. Then she raised the bullhorn to her mouth once more and announced, "Ladies and gentlemen, and all of you media-type persons, if I might have your attention? I've just seen that Logan Callahan of Callahan and Son, architects for the building to be erected here, is among us. I've spoken to Mr. Callahan at some length about Sandler House and, indeed, we've both toured it just this week. Mr. Callahan, would you please come up here and tell us what we discovered?" She turned, pointed in his direction. "Mr. Callahan, ladies and gentlemen."

Logan dipped his head for a moment, then lifted it again, still grinning at her. He raised his hand in acknowledgement, then made his way through the crowd, a crowd that parted for him as everyone watched the tall, denim-clad man lazily make his way across the field, onto the construction road.

"I'm going to kiss you senseless for this, Dawson," he breathed into her ear as he joined her.

"I love you, too," she responded, then wished she could drop through a hole in the ground as she heard her own voice blasting out over the crowd via the bullhorn she'd forgotten to turn off.

Women laughed, men chuckled, and Carl Whittier looked at her as if she were a traitor to humanity.

Smiling a smile of the sort that had gotten generations of women in trouble over the centuries, Logan took the bullhorn from her and greeted the crowd, thanking them all for coming out for his announcement.

"Announcement?" Ashley asked, pushing the bullhorn away from his face. "What announcement? Callahan, what are you talking about?"

"We'll never know, will we, dear," Bonnie Kauffman pointed out reasonably, adjusting her pith helmet, "if you don't let him speak."

"I'm going to tell everyone our plans for Sandler House," Logan told her, trying to retrieve the bullhorn.

"That's it? You're just going to stand here and baldly announce that you're reducing it to rubble, hail progress, thank you so much now go away? Are you *nuts?* Let me handle this."

Showing all the signs of being an obedient sort— which should have been Ashley's first clue—he stepped back, bowed, and let her have at it.

"Ladies and gentlemen, Mr. Callahan has been very kind and understanding so far, even though we're trespassing on private property. He has also, earlier this week and at my request, taken me on a tour of Sandler House, at which time we saw the extent of the damage weather, vandals and just plain age have done to the building. As a representative of the Historical Society, I can tell you with some certainty that even if we could gain deed to the property there is no possible way we could ever restore Sandler House to its former glory.''

"Yes there is."

Ashley stood very still for a moment, then swiveled her head in Logan's direction. "What did you say?"

"I said," Logan repeated, taking the bullhorn from her, speaking through it, "after consultation with contractors, after speaking to my client who has been agreeable to seeing the historic and public relations benefits to preserving Sandler House, we have decided that, yes, the building can be saved.''

"You're kidding. When did this happen—and why didn't you tell me?" Ashley breathed, her knees a little weak.

"Nope, three days ago, and you didn't ask, actually," he told her, his smile so proud she longed to wipe it straight off his mouth. With her mouth. "Now, do you want to know how, or do you want to interrupt me again?"

She pushed both her hands at him, wordlessly signaling that he had the floor, so why didn't he go ahead and speak. Besides, she didn't think she could say anything else if someone put a gun to her head and told her to recite her own name, address, and phone number. Her brain, frankly, had gone on stun.

"Fellas?" Logan shouted, putting down the bullhorn, which really was more trouble than it was worth. "Are you ready?"

One of the construction workers raised his hand in acknowledgement. So that's why they were there. They were Callahan's men. They started walking to

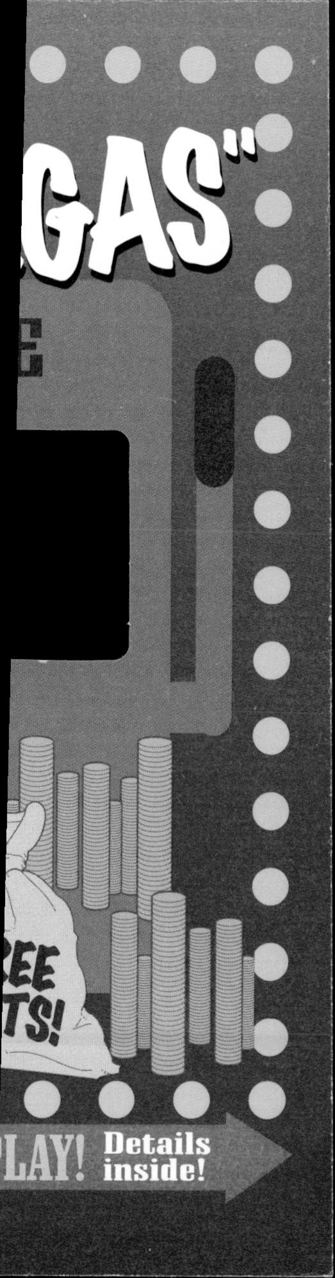
Details
inside!

Play the

"LAS

3 FRE

FREE
GIFTS!

1. Pull back all 3 tabs on t
   see what we have for you
   FREE!

2. Send back this card and
   novels. These books hav
   $3.99 each in Canada, b

3. There's no catch. You're
   nothing — ZERO — for
   any minimum number o

4. The fact is thousands of
   Silhouette Reader Service
   they like getting the best
   and they love our discou

5. We hope that after receiv
   subscriber. But the choic
   all! So why not take us u
   You'll be glad you did!

FREE!
No Obligation to Buy!
No Purchase Necessary!

Play the

"LAS VEGAS"
Game

PEEL BACK HERE ▶
PEEL BACK HERE ▶
PEEL BACK HERE ▶

YES! I have pulled back the 3 tabs. Please send me all the free Silhouette Romance® books and the gift for which I qualify. I understand that I am under no obligation to purchase any books, as explained on the back and opposite page.

315 SDL C23W   **215 SDL C23S**

NAME   (PLEASE PRINT CLEARLY)

ADDRESS

APT.#   CITY

STATE/PROV.   ZIP/POSTAL CODE

  GET 2 FREE BOOKS & A FREE MYSTERY GIFT!

 GET 2 FREE BOOKS!

 GET 1 FREE BOOK!

  TRY AGAIN!

DETACH AND MAIL TODAY ▼

If offer card is missing write to: Silhouette Reader Service, 3010 Walden Ave., P.O. Box 1867, Buffalo, NY 14240-1867

BUSINESS REPLY MAIL
FIRST-CLASS MAIL   PERMIT NO. 717   BUFFALO, NY

POSTAGE WILL BE PAID BY ADDRESSEE

SILHOUETTE READER SERVICE
3010 WALDEN AVE
PO BOX 1867
BUFFALO NY 14240-9952

NO POSTAGE
NECESSARY
IF MAILED
IN THE
UNITED STATES

their left, and that's when Ashley finally saw the two tarpaulin-covered signs stuck into the ground with wooden legs.

She looked at the tarps, looked at Logan, and then just stood back and watched. Listened.

"Ladies and gentlemen, Barrows Electronics has agreed to let me announce their decision to *move* Sandler House to the site where you'll see two signs we've erected to mark its destination. This is quite a large, expensive project, and will delay the beginning of construction, so you can understand that I'm very proud of Barrows Electronics for their generous spirit in all of this. The plan is to completely refurbish the building to its original glory, and use it as the new home of the day-care center for all Barrows employees."

The cheer that went up was deafening, because now everyone was happy. Even Carl Whittier.

"You're kidding."

"Not right now I'm not, Ashley honey. But if you want me to *amuse* you later," he said, winking at her, "I'm game if you are. Now hang on a moment, I'm not done."

He picked up the bullhorn again, a necessary tool now, and requested that the construction workers remove the tarp covering one of the large signs, revealing an artist's drawing of Sandler House—sans front porch—and the information that this spot would become its new home.

More cheering. More grinning. More of Ashley trying very hard to keep her jaw from dropping onto the ground.

"And now, ladies and gentlemen, if you'll bear

with me a moment longer—guys, the second sign, if
you please?''

He turned to Ashley, slid his arm around her waist.
''I thought we'd do this tomorrow, a little more pri-
vately, but we're here now, so I figured why not go
for it all in one big flourish.''

''Go for what? I don't under—ohmi*gawd!* Callahan, you *idiot!*''

The construction workers had pulled the tarp from
the sign, exposing—in rather lurid pink lettering—
the simple lines: Ashley, I Love You. Marry Me?
Callahan.

''Well, that's tacky,'' Carl Whittier said, pushing
his way through the crowd in order to make his exit.

Ashley didn't hear him, or notice all the clicking
cameras, as she was altogether too caught up in Logan's kiss.

The morning after their marriage which, coinci-
dentally, also happened to be the morning after that
rather public proposal, Ashley and Logan Callahan
sat across a linen-covered table, enjoying their breakfast and a view of the Las Vegas strip from the comfort of their hotel suite.

''So the architect simply *assumed* the building
would be demolished?''

Logan dipped a strawberry into whipped cream,
offered it to Ashley. It just wasn't a cornflakes-and-
toast kind of morning.

''Correct. The cost of the demolition was figured
into the costs, but I'd never gone over the costs in
that much detail, which is my fault. Klein had
checked the building's historical significance, found

nothing that would make him think anyone would object to the demolition or that we would be opening up the can of worms we ended up opening up, then submitted the plans—sans Sandler House. We've had a little talk, Klein and me. It won't happen again.''

Ashley wiped her mouth with her napkin, sat back against her chair, shaking her head. "I don't know, darling. I think we ought to write the guy a thank-you note. I mean, if it weren't for the mix up, we'd never have met. Have I mentioned yet this morning how very much I love you, Mr. Callahan?''

"Twice, but we can go for three, Mrs. Callahan," he told her, already half rising from his chair as the phone began to ring. "I'll get that, although I can't imagine who it is. Nobody knows we're here, right?''

"Callahan," Ashley said, shaking her head as she, too, rose, and headed for the phone. "Do you really think I could leave town without first warning Mary? If Mom called and I didn't answer? Well, I don't want to think about that." She picked up the phone, smiled at Logan, then said, "Good morning, Mom. How long did it take you to track us down?''

She listened for a while, as Lindsay Dawson rather proudly described the phone calls she'd been making all morning in her attempt to locate her eloping daughter.

"Are you happy, sweetheart?" Lindsay asked at last. "Really, *really* happy?''

Ashley sat down on the bed, barely suppressing a satisfied moan as Logan began nuzzling her neck. "Yes, Mom, I'm happy. Delirious, actually. Do you mind very much not having to plan another wedding? After Mary's, you did say you didn't even want to think about another wedding reception for a few years.''

She listened again, slapping at Logan's hands as he began tickling her, then said goodbye to her mother and hung up the phone. "She's happy, thrilled, and calling your dad to arrange a *small* reception for us in about a month. She told me Mary faxed her the story in the morning paper—there's a picture of us, by the way—and then told me our elopement is just about the most romantic thing she's ever heard and she's betting you're going to be a wonderful husband and son-in-law. That's my mom, really a sweetheart. So, that's settled. Now, how about you tell me you love me. I don't think I'll ever tire of hearing it.''

Logan took hold of her shoulders, eased her down on the mattress, almost kissed her. Almost, because suddenly he was sitting up, staring down at her. "Your mother is calling my father? When will she be talking to him?''

"When he answers the phone, silly,'' Ashley said, also sitting up. "What's the matter? Don't tell me you haven't called your father yet, haven't told him we're married?''

"No, no, I put a call in to his hotel, but he'd checked out yesterday. The desk clerk said he was taking a flight back to the States, which figures, as he never takes vacations, doesn't know the meaning of the word *relax*. Damn! How many times have I told him his name and home number shouldn't be listed in the telephone directory? If your mother talks to him before I can get hold of him…''

"It's Sunday, Callahan, so relax. Mom said something about phoning him at his office tomorrow morning, not at home. You'll get hold of him before then, won't you? Besides, this is *good* news. Isn't it?''

"Good news? It's the *best* news," he told her, easing her back onto the bed, resuming his slow, gentle seduction. "So, how do you feel about ten days in Italy, now that we're all legal and everything?"

"Callahan?" Ashley asked, eying him carefully. "Are you *afraid* of your father?"

"Nope," he assured her, unbuttoning her blouse, kissing the exposed skin. "But Dad has this thing about impulsive decisions. I think we might want to give him some time to get used to this one. Now, come here, Mrs. Callahan, and let's concentrate on our honeymoon. I'm figuring we can make it last, oh, fifty or sixty years."

"I like the way you think," she told him, and then they didn't talk again for a long time.

But the giggles were nice....

* * * * *

Be sure to watch for Kasey Michaels'
new trilogy coming to Silhouette Romance
this September.

"Ryan Objects"

Joan Hohl

Books by Joan Hohl

Silhouette Romance

A Taste for Rich Things #334
Someone Waiting #358
The Scent of Lilacs #376
Carried Away #1438

Silhouette Desire

A Much Needed Holiday #247
*Texas Gold #294
**California Copper* #312
*Nevada Silver #330
Lady Ice #354
One Tough Hombre #372
Falcon's Flight #390
The Gentleman Insists #475
Christmas Stranger #540
Handsome Devil #612
Convenient Husband #732
Lyon's Cub #762
†*Wolfe Waiting* #806
†*Wolfe Watching* #865
†*Wolfe Wanting* #884
†*Wolfe Wedding* #973
A Memorable Man #1075

*Desire Trilogy
†Big, Bad Wolfe Series

Silhouette Special Edition

Thorne's Way #54
Forever Spring #444
Thorne's Wife #537

Silhouette Intimate Moments

*Moments Harsh,
  Moments Gentle* #35

Silhouette Books

†*Wolfe Winter*

Silhouette Summer Sizzlers 1988
"Grand Illusion"

Silhouette Christmas Stories 1993
"Holiday Homecoming"

Silhouette Summer Sizzlers 1996
"Gone Fishing"

JOAN HOHL

is the bestselling author of almost three dozen books. She has received numerous awards for her work, including the Romance Writers of America's Golden Medallion award. In addition to contemporary romance, this prolific author also writes historical and time-travel romances. Joan lives in eastern Pennsylvania with her husband and family.

Chapter One

Ryan Callahan simmered with repressed but rapidly escalating angry impatience as he listened to the light, bubbly female voice on the tape replaying on his office answering machine.

The woman had introduced herself as one Lindsay Dawson who, as of two days ago according to her, had become the mother-in-law of Ryan's business partner and only child, his son, Logan...the impetuous fool.

The voice was pleasant, low, kind of throaty, one might even say sexy—if one were of a mind to do so, which Ryan definitely was not.

Logan? Ryan questioned in silent fury. Married? How? When? Why, for Pete's sake? Hell, he'd never heard of this Dawson woman, let alone her daughter. If what the woman was saying was true, why hadn't Logan said something when he'd called Ryan at his hotel in Tokyo a week ago? Yet, all Logan had said was that he needed a break, a vacation. He'd never even mentioned a woman named Ashley.

Tamping down a startling and unwelcome surge of interest, and even more disturbing, a spark of sensual response, he ground his teeth as the sultry voice sang on, providing the answers to the question stinging his mind.

"...so, while I accepted Ashley's and Logan's decision to forego a more conventional and formal wedding by so unexpectedly eloping to Las Vegas two days ago—they obviously are so very much in love, you know—"

No, he didn't know anything of the sort, Ryan railed, but before he could give voice to his expanding ire in the form of a string of curses, she gaily continued singing away.

"—I insisted on them allowing me—and, of course, you, if you wish—to plan a small reception for them when they return from their honeymoon."

Ryan's back teeth were now clamped together so tightly, sharp pains were shooting into his rigid jaw. If he wished? he thought, grimacing. He damn well did not wish to involve himself in the planning of a belated wedding reception for the two young idiots. What he did wish was that Logan were there, standing in front of him, so Ryan could vent his anger by tearing a verbal strip off of his son's hide for his reckless and impulsive act. Come to that, he wouldn't mind the opportunity to say a few choice words to the apparently bubble-headed young Ashley, as well.

Ryan's eyes narrowed as Lindsay Dawson's voice blithely ran on, confidently reciting her home and business phone and fax numbers, e-mail address for both, and the location in the King of Prussia Plaza mall of her store, Lindsay's Intimates...whatever that might be.

"...and I'm so looking forward to meeting you," she ended, finally running down and disconnecting.

Oh, for certain, Mrs. Dawson would be meeting him, Ryan mused, scowling at the now silent answering machine. But he seriously doubted she would enjoy the meeting, for if she thought for one second he would willingly fall in with her plans, Lindsay Dawson had another thought coming. The absolute last thing Ryan felt inclined to do was to celebrate the hasty marriage of his boneheaded son to her very likely fluff-brained daughter.

It wasn't that Ryan was opposed to marriage as an institution, exactly. Some of his best friends were married, although, offhand, he couldn't name many who appeared either happy or content within the confines of the state.

But Ryan had been there, done that, and every bit as ill-considered and precipitously as Logan...and had paid the price demanded for his passionate impulsiveness.

No, it wasn't the marriage per se that Ryan was opposed to. For all he knew, this Ashley, née Dawson, now Callahan, was a very nice young woman.

On the other hand, for all he knew, she could very well turn out to be a flyaway, self-centered, all-for-me-and-the-hell-with-everybody-else witch. A physically attractive, vain young woman cast from the same mold as the woman Ryan had married in lusting haste before he'd been out of his teens, and with whom at the age of twenty he had produced one child, his son.

So, it wasn't that Ryan thought the twenty-seven-year-old Logan was too young to marry, but that he feared the union might have been built on the slippery slope of passionate haste, and doomed to failure, as his own had been.

Considering the fact that Ryan had never heard his son mention the girl's name, the too real possibility of a similar scenario in Logan's case actually frightened Ryan, and when Ryan was frightened, he got mad.

After hearing the elder Dawson's chatty message, Ryan was doing a slow burn. For a moment, he felt tempted to drop everything, drive to King of Prussia, find the woman's store, and demand some answers to the questions raised by her brief message.

Questions such as:

When had his son and her daughter met?

How long had they known each other?

Why had they decided to marry so precipitously, without even bothering to inform him?

And exactly where in the hell were they staying in Las Vegas, anyway?

Feeling a need to know everything, Ryan reached across his desk for the intercom to summon his secretary. He was planning to tell her to clear his schedule for the day, when his glance landed on the stacks of mail and other papers that had piled up on his desk during his absence.

Heaving a frustrated sigh, he drew his hand back. His questions and his visit to Mrs. Sultry-voiced

Dawson would have to wait; he had a lot of catching up to do.

Ryan had made inroads into the stack of mail when his phone buzzed, indicating the caller was someone his secretary would put through without his prior consent. Thinking it might be Logan, he snatched up the receiver.

"Callahan," he said, in a near snarl.

"Good morning to you, too," his son returned, his pleasant voice abrading Ryan's simmering anger. "Rough trip?"

"Damn it, Logan," he barked into the receiver, ignoring his son's greeting and his question. "What the hell have you gone and done?"

There was a pause, a sigh. "You've already talked to Mrs. Dawson," he said.

"No, I haven't talked to her," Ryan said. "She left a message on my answering machine."

"So did I."

Ryan frowned. There had been several messages on his office machine, none of them from his son. "When? There was no message here from you."

"Not there," Logan said. "I left a message yesterday, on your home machine."

"Damn." Ryan grunted. "I didn't play back the tape on my home machine," he said. "To answer your question, yes, it was a rough trip, not business-wise, but the flight home. As you know, I was supposed to have a short layover at O'Hare, for a change of planes. But a series of violent storms delayed all flights. I was stuck there in the airport for over twelve hours."

"Bummer," Logan inserted.

"Tell me about it." Recalled agitation edged his voice. "I didn't get home until after seven yesterday morning. After disconnecting my bedroom phone jack, I hit the sack, slept the clock around. I was late into the office, that's why I missed Mrs. Dawson's call."

"And why you didn't play back your home machine messages," Logan concluded.

"Yes...but that doesn't change the fact that you were calling to present me with a fait accompli, does it?" Ryan demanded. "And without saying a word to me before running off like a fool kid."

"I did try to tell you, Dad," Logan explained himself. "I called your hotel in Tokyo. The desk clerk told me you had already left for the airport."

"That's no excuse," Ryan snapped. "Damn it, Logan, have you lost your mind?"

"No, Dad, I lost my heart. I fell in love." Logan's soft, tender tones made Ryan's hackles rise.

"When?" he asked, none too gently. "Damn, Logan, I leave town for a couple of weeks and you go off the rails."

"Dad, I didn't go..." That's as far as he got before Ryan cut in to pepper him with questions.

"Why haven't you ever mentioned this woman? Who is she? Where does she come from? Why haven't I met her? When are you coming home?"

"I haven't mentioned her before, because I just recently met her myself," Logan said, his own voice now edgy as he shot back his answers. "She comes from Allentown. You haven't met her because you were out of the country. And we won't be home for a couple of weeks because we're flying to Newark tomorrow morning to catch a flight for Rome."

"And you can't stop off in Philadelphia first?" Ryan came as close as he ever did to shouting.

"We could...but we're not going to. We're on our honeymoon, remember?" Logan came close to shouting back, proving he was his father's son. "And, Dad, her name is Ashley, not her or she, but Ashley." Further proof. "Get used to it, because I love her, and I'm planning to hang on to her for the rest of my life."

"Brave words," Ryan retorted.

"I'm a brave man," Logan volleyed. "I take after my father, the bravest man I know. The smartest, too. Which reminds me. Did you secure the Hoshi contract for Callahan and Son?"

"Yes, the contract's a done deal," Ryan answered, his lips curing into a wry smile at his son's blatant flattery. "And compliments get you nothing."

Logan laughed. "It was worth a shot."

Ryan's smile widened, though he was glad Logan couldn't see it. But, damn, he did love this son of his. He cleared his throat. "What about the Barrows Electronics project?"

"Everything's under control."

"Good. Now, about this so-called marriage of yours," Ryan said, returning to the original, worrisome subject.

"Er...later, Dad. Plenty of time for explanations after we get back from Italy," Logan said in a rush. "I can't talk any longer, we have to leave for the airport. Bye."

"Logan," Ryan barked, recalling their conversation of the previous week.

A sigh. "Yes, Dad?"

"Your hand." His voice betrayed concern. "Is it all right."

"Yes, Dad, it's fine." Logan's low tone was soft with affection. "Now, please say goodbye and let me hang up, so Ashley and I can get going."

Ryan sighed as he cradled the receiver. Logan was a man, capable of making his own decisions, but damned if Ryan could accept this quick plunge into marriage. He was afraid Logan had just taken the first steps along the same disastrous path he himself had trod twenty-eight years ago. He'd have thought Logan knew better. He certainly had tried to teach him the folly of acting in haste.

Impetuous fools, both of them, Logan and Ashley. The thought refueled Ryan's anger. For a moment, he again gave serious consideration to ignoring the work on his desk and driving to King of Prussia to unleash his frustration on Ashley's mother, the sole member of the Dawson family within his reach. But habit and better judgment prevailed; Ryan attacked the mound of paperwork.

It was after five-thirty when Ryan left his center city office complex. The intervening hours had not gone far in appeasing his anger. The rush-hour traffic streaming west along the Schuylkill Expressway ratcheted up his irritation. By the time he took the exit to King of Prussia, his stomach felt hollow, tied in knots.

Or maybe he was hungry. Ryan frowned, only then realizing that he hadn't stopped working to eat lunch, hadn't even thought about food. Now it was almost dinnertime.

Dinner. Damn. Ryan grimaced. He had completely forgotten that he had a dinner engagement—a formal, social affair in honor of local artists and local businessmen and women for their patronage of the arts.

The dinner was for eight. Ryan spared a glance for the dashboard clock. 6:05. He'd be pressed. Shrugging, he directed the car into the mall parking lot. Once he found the woman's shop, how long could it take? Finding a slot, he left the car and headed to the nearest entrance.

The floor directory provided the location of Lindsay's Intimates. His stride determined, Ryan set out to find and confront the woman, fully prepared to fire a few scathing missiles to shoot down the excitement-riddled, throaty-voiced Lindsay Dawson's reception bubbles.

Ryan located the store without difficulty. He paused, one dark eyebrow arched, to examine the merchandise displayed in the show window.

Lingerie. Lindsay's Intimates. He should have known. But not just any everyday lingerie. Oh, no, Ryan mused, noting the obvious quality of the merchandise.

Sauntering inside, his gaze made a slow sweep of the stock, folded neatly on display tables, hanging on racks strategically positioned on the available floor space and against the walls, and draped to advantage on a few curvaceous mannequins, most of the filmy bits of satin and lace revealing more than they concealed.

Ryan was the sole male inside the store, and yet

he didn't feel in the least uncomfortable or embarrassed. Strolling toward the sales counter, he studied the variety of garments on offer with a practiced eye. Having been a bachelor for twenty-six years, and being a healthy, normal male not inclined toward celibacy, he had seen, touched, removed his share of alluring underthings.

Maybe he was old-fashioned, he reflected, his gaze skimming over the more revealing pieces before settling for a moment on a rather demure, but in his estimation much more provocative nightgown and negligée ensemble displayed in a small separate section labeled For The Bride. The set was of cotton, fine but not see-through sheer—white, flowing, tantalizing.

Under the right circumstances and adorning the right woman, he could become very aroused by slowly, sensuously removing those two enticing pieces of fluff, Ryan thought, a wry smile teasing his lips.

It occurred to him that the woman had at least one point in her favor; Mrs. Chatty Dawson had excellent taste...at least in so far as her merchandise went.

The thought recalled his purpose in being there, the only man in the store, in the first place. Dismissing the stock, his gaze homed in on the counter.

A saleswoman stood behind it, bagging a customer's dainty, transparent purchases. Ignoring the young customer and the unmentionables, he evaluated the saleswoman.

Obviously not the owner, Ryan decided, taking a closer, appreciative look at the woman. Thirty-something, he figured. About a foot shorter than his own six-two, but every inch packed solid with feminine allure. Russet-shaded hair. Dark, dark eyes, probably bittersweet chocolate brown, the kind that used to be called bedroom eyes. Delicate features, encased in fine, satiny-looking skin. Creamy complexion.

Ryan experienced an unexpected and surprising jolt of physical response—unexpected because a sexual reaction had been the last thing on his mind; surprising because it had been some long months since he had felt a similar sensation.

Damn. He didn't have time for dalliance, Ryan told himself. He had a *mother* to contend with.

So where in hell was the woman, anyway? He didn't have all night; he had a dinner to attend.

Even as the grousing thought flitted through Ryan's mind, another clerk, older, more matronly in appearance, rounded the counter to take command of the register.

Ah-hah, the mother.

The older woman spoke to the other clerk. Thirty-something nodded and flashed a smile.

Oh, have mercy, Ryan thought, muscles clenching against a hunger unrelated to his empty stomach.

Thirty-something of the teeth-melting smile stepped to a door set in the wall a few feet behind the register. Ryan cut a quick, encompassing glance over her well-rounded form, clothed to advantage in a neat navy blue pin-striped suit and tailored crisp white shirt.

The clenching sensation expanding inside, Ryan strode up to the counter.

"May I help you, sir?" The older woman's voice

was polite, pleasant, but unremarkable, not at all like the sultry yet effervescent tones on his answering machine.

"I hope so," Ryan said, frowning at the sudden certainty that this wasn't the woman he sought. "I'm looking for Mrs. Lindsay Dawson."

"I'm Lindsay Dawson," the younger woman said, turning from the door she had opened.

She most definitely was, Ryan thought, feeling another jolt of response. He'd have recognized her voice anywhere.

"What can I do for you?" She smiled.

Ryan stifled a groan. In that instant, he could think of many things she could do for him, not least of which was model that white negligée ensemble, and not one of which pertained to some harebrained scheme for a wedding reception.

"We need to talk," he said in tones roughened by self-impatience and suppressed anger, at himself for his stupid response to her, and unreasonably in the extreme, at her for causing the response. Damned inconvenient.

"We do?" Perfectly arched eyebrows rose over dark brown eyes sparked by inner amusement. "What about?"

"I'm Ryan Callahan," he said with blunt authority, as if that explained everything, which of course, it did.

An infinitesimal pause, surprise, and then her eyes widened, her smile dazzled, and her distinctive voice tantalized his senses. "Logan's father."

"Yes…" His voice lowered to a self-protective growl. "Logan's father."

She glanced around, noting, as Ryan did, the interested curiosity on the older woman's face. "We can't talk here, we'd be in Betty's way," she said, smiling nicely at the woman. "I...er, was just leaving to go to dinner. Would you care to join me?"

Leading question, if he ever heard one. His revitalized libido was signaling willingness to join her in the most basic of ways. Disgusted with his juvenile reaction to her, Ryan gave himself a mental shake. He was about to reflect the motion with his head, decline her invitation, but like quicksilver, changed his mind.

So he had a dinner engagement. Big deal. The food, he knew from experience, would be so-so. The place would be packed with other businessmen and women, most with companions. He wouldn't be missed. Nor would he be disappointing a date as, unsure if he'd be back from Japan in time for the affair, he hadn't invited anyone to accompany him.

"Of course," she inserted into his rapid-fire thoughts. "If you have other plans..." Her voice trailed off.

"No." He shook his head, the decision made. "Did you have any particular place in mind?"

"Well...no." She shrugged, causing the clench to really dig into his gut with the movement of her full breasts. "But there are plenty of restaurants in the area."

"Wherever," Ryan said, his shoulders mirroring her motion. "So long as it's quiet and the food's good."

She frowned in obvious consideration of the selection of restaurants available.

"There's the Drop Inn over near your complex," Betty suggested, smiling at Ryan. "The atmosphere is always quiet and conducive to conversation, and the food's first-rate."

"Oh, I never thought of the Inn." Lindsay Dawson flashed that melting smile. "Thank you, Betty." She turned the smile on him, making Ryan fear for the enamel on his teeth. "If that's all right with you?"

"Sounds fine," he said, ready to agree to any place just to get out of there and pull himself together. "If you'll point me in the right direction?"

Minutes later, Ryan retraced his recent path back to his car, lecturing himself in time with his rapid steps. The woman was married, he reminded himself, in an effort to quash the feeling of anticipation sizzling inside him. She was a mother, the mother of the woman now married to his son.

She didn't look old enough to be the mother of anybody's daughter-in-law. She certainly didn't look anything near what he had been expecting.

Damn.

We need to talk.

The raspy, impatient sound of his voice echoing in her head, Lindsay slid behind the wheel of her compact car and sat still for long moments, staring at the tremor in her fingers clutching the car keys.

The outward tremor reflected an inner shimmer, a tingling excitement teasing her senses, skipping along her central nervous system.

Ryan Callahan.

Thinking his name intensified the tingling sensation. An image of him formed in her mind of the way he'd looked on her first sight of him. His expression set in lines of determination, he had approached the counter like a man on a mission, primed and prepared for battle.

And Ryan Callahan was prime, all six feet two inches give or take of toned muscles and rugged, sexy good looks. Hazel eyes glittering, masculine in the extreme, he literally radiated the impression of a fire-breathing sight to set the heart, and libido, of any young-, middle- or old-aged red-blooded woman to quivering. And, from the fierce look of him, he appeared angry enough to spit nails.

His overall appearance had put Lindsay in mind of the tall, ruggedly handsome, grimly determined warrior hero pictured in just about every historical novel she had ever read, and she had read many. Only, instead of a military uniform, or pirate's garb, or armor, or the Highland plaid, Ryan Callahan's imposing body had been encased in a perfectly tailored suit bearing a famous label.

He intimidated and excited Lindsay at the same time.

Trembling hands gripping the steering wheel, she chided and chastised herself all the way to the restaurant.

What is this? Lindsay asked herself, mindful of the early evening traffic. She hadn't experienced this quivery, churning, breathless sensation since her high school days, and then never to this degree.

Good grief, Ryan Callahan was only a man, she reminded herself. What's more, he was a man crowding fifty, silver threads woven through the short strands of dark hair at his temples, certainly not a bold young warrior.

Good thing, too, she thought with a short, nervous bubble of laughter. She wouldn't have the vaguest idea how to deal with a bold young warrior. Playing the heroine was not her style. She was too reserved, content with her everyday life.

At age forty-four, Lindsay considered herself relatively young, certainly young enough to continue on in the career niche she had carved out for herself in retail sales in order to supplement her income, support herself and her two young daughters, after the death of her husband.

But Lindsay also considered herself mature, past the age of thrilling to the appearance of a man, any man. While intellectually she understood sexual attraction, she didn't trust it, so didn't indulge herself with it. She had put that particular kind of involvement behind her after a brief, unconsumated alliance with a contemporary of her husband's a few years after her husband's untimely death.

And she definitely wasn't about to reverse course at this stage of her life.

Which was all rather academic, Lindsay thought with wry humor as she drove onto the parking lot at the Inn, since Ryan Callahan had appeared more in the mood for a fight then in an attempt at seduction.

Lindsay was smiling as she left the car and made her way to the restaurant entrance. The quivery excitement inside had calmed, the tremor in her fingers stilled.

She was adept at dealing with the occasional disgruntled customers, male as well as female. She could handle her daughter's irate father-in-law.

Callahan was waiting for her at the door, his tall form bathed in golden light from the westering early evening spring sun rays.

The sight of him robbed Lindsay of breath, reactivated the quivery excitement, set her fingers trembling.

Darn the man.

Chapter Two

"They're holding a table for us." Ryan pulled the door open and stepped back, motioning her to precede him inside.

The hostess, an attractive blond woman in her late twenties or early thirties, greeted them with a sparkling smile...that is, she greeted Ryan with the smile, while barely acknowledging Lindsay's presence.

Undecided whether to laugh or feel offended, Lindsay did neither, but simply followed the woman to a secluded table off to one side of the dining room, near a window looking out over a patio, now empty, and a small side garden resplendent with spring blooms and flowering trees.

After proffering large menus, the woman favored Ryan with another interest-proclaiming smile. "Your server will be with you in a moment," she confided, again to Ryan. "Enjoy your dinner."

Annoyed with her obviousness and rudeness,

Lindsay was glad to see the back of the woman once more as she walked away. So, apparently, was Ryan, for different reasons, if the speculative perusal he gave her swaying hips was any indication to the direction of his thoughts.

Men.

Now more than annoyed, and confused as to why she should even care, Lindsay raised the menu to conceal her expression of any traces of the disdain she was feeling for the male species, and their susceptibly to being so easily engaged by a pretty face and twitching bottom.

"Anything appeal?"

Lindsay peered over the top rim of the menu at him, a curl of something unfurling inside at the shadowed, slumberous look in the hazel eyes regarding her.

In the next moment, the curl curled up and died, as Ryan's gaze shifted to observe the passage of the hostess as she glided past their table with new patrons in tow.

"The broiled salmon in dill," Lindsay answered, refraining from commenting that it was obvious the hostess had more appeal to him than the food selections.

"Hmm." The hostess now out of sight, he returned his attention to the menu. "I'm not in the mood for fish."

Cynically certain she knew exactly what he was in the mood for, Lindsay was sorely tempted to reach across the table and whack him with the large pasteboard bill of fare. However, appalled at herself for her unusual aggressive impulse, she contained the

militant urge and carefully set the prospective
weapon aside.

"I'm going to have the steak."

The steak. Of course, Lindsay mused. Red meat,
very likely rare, the choice of virile men.

Honestly.

"Good evening." The server, fortunately male,
middle-aged with a benign smile, halted beside the
table. "Can I get you a drink from the bar...or coffee?"

"Yes, thank you." Lindsay gave her attention, and
a smile to the pleasant-voiced man. "Since I'm driving, I'll have coffee, just cream, please."

"What beer do you have on tap?" Ryan asked,
ignoring her pointed hint about drinking and driving.

The waiter rattled off a list of some well-known
brands, plus a few micro brews, along with their dis-
tinctions.

"Raspberry?" Ryan pronounced the word in tones
of near revulsion, then went on to order a brand
name, light, to Lindsay's relief.

"Very good, sir." Collecting the menus, the
waiter departed to get their order.

Silence.

Suddenly uncomfortable alone at the table with
this man she didn't know, but was already sure she
wasn't going to like if she ever did get to know him,
Lindsay glanced down, busying her hands with
spreading her napkin over her lap.

"So, how do you really feel about it?"

Lindsay blinked and looked up, startled by the
abrupt, rough sound of his voice, as well as the ques-

tion. "How do I really feel about what—raspberry flavoring in a micro brew?"

"Of course not." Impatience laced his voice, flickered in his eyes. "I'm referring to this ill-conceived, headlong rush into matrimony by my son and your daughter."

Lindsay's spine stiffened as she sat up board straight in the chair. "While I admit that Ashley and Logan's decision to marry was a bit hasty..." that was as far as he allowed her to go before cutting her off.

"A bit hasty?" he demanded in mocking tones. "I'd say it was damned hasty, not to mention stupid."

Had he actually said that his son and *her* daughter were stupid? Oh, without doubt, Lindsay fumed, she was not going to like him no matter how well she might be forced to know him, deal with him.

"Mr. Callahan," she began, her ice-coated voice reflecting her cold expression. But before she could continue, the waiter appeared at the table.

"Your drinks," he said, setting a cup in front of her and a tall pilsner glass in front of her adversary. "Are you ready to order your dinner?"

Her appetite gone, Lindsay hesitated.

Ryan didn't. "The lady will have the broiled salmon. I'll have the Delmonico, medium."

"Sides?" The waiter asked.

Ryan leveled a pointed look at her.

"Baked potato and the tossed garden salad... house dressing," Lindsay said, smiling up at the waiter through her clenched teeth.

"I'll have the same."

"Thank you." The waiter again took his leave.

Dreading being alone once more with the unfriendly man opposite her, Lindsay turned to gaze out the window.

"Ryan."

The low, commanding sound of his voice drew her sharpened, wary gaze back to him. "I beg your pardon?"

He smiled, drawing her attention to his mouth, the masculine thinness of his sculpted upper lip, the hint of sensuous fullness of the lower. A shiver of blatant sexual awareness sent a wave of heat through her. Her throat suddenly parched, she grasped the coffee cup, raised it to her lips, and despite the scorching warmth, emptied it in a few deep swallows. It didn't help. In fact, it burned liked the very devil. She followed the coffee with a gulp of iced water.

"I said, my name is Ryan...Lindsay." His softened tone sent a thrilling chill chasing the wave of heat through her. Mirroring her action, he polished off his beer. "Don't you think, since—thanks to our respective offspring—we apparently are now all one big happy family, we can dispense with the formalities?" He arched one dark eyebrow in mocking punctuation.

Having not as yet met the man her daughter had married, and claimed to be deliriously in love with, Lindsay had no way of knowing that the one arched eyebrow that Ryan used to such effect—and she had felt the effect—was one of the few mannerisms father and son shared. Except, in Logan's case, it was the left eyebrow, having acquired the habit, quite unconsciously, while facing his father, reflecting his action.

Lindsay felt duly mocked, and none too pleased about it, either. "I suppose," she answered in grudging agreement, not bothering to conceal her displeasure. "But then, don't you think...Ryan," she gritted his name, "since we are now one big happy family, it is a little unkind to refer to our respective offspring as being stupid?" she asked, tossing his words back at him.

"I didn't say *they* were stupid...Lindsay," he retorted. "I said their rash action was stupid."

"But they are in love," she blurted out in defense of the absent couple.

"Or in lust," he shot back at her. "History records that some of the most intelligent of people have been know to rush their fences while in the throes of lust." He gave a short, self-deprecating laugh. "I myself am living proof of the truth of it."

Comprehension dawned over the horizon of Lindsay's mind. "You married in haste?"

His smile was wry, his nod sharp. "And, in tried-and-true fashion, repented in leisure, both before and after the divorce less than two years later."

"I see. And that's why you're so angry now." It wasn't a question; Lindsay already knew the answer.

"You're damned right," he answered, anyway. "I'm amazed that you are not. Isn't your husband?"

"I'm a widow, Ryan," Lindsay said with cautionary reluctance, certain he'd pounce on the fact to undermine her in some way. To her surprise, he did not.

He sighed. "I'm sorry. Recent?"

"No." She shook her head. "It's been almost twenty years." Now she sighed, but went on in all honesty, "But, I admit that, were he still alive, and knowing him for the caring, protective man he was, Jeffrey would probably be every bit as angry and upset as you are now."

"Then, why aren't you?" he asked in tones smoothed of the abrasive edges. "Don't you care?"

"Of course I care," she cried out softly in protest. "But I also trust my daughter, her common sense."

"Common sense?" He laughed in ridicule. "What common sense do you see displayed by either Logan or Ashley in this? How long have they known each other?"

Lindsay lowered her eyes from the intensity of his, hesitant to answer for fear of really setting him off.

"You might as well tell me," he said, correctly reading her trepidation. "I'll find out sooner or later."

Wishing it could be much later, Lindsay cleared her throat, swallowed, and muttered, "A week."

"A week?" He exclaimed, drawing several curious glances their way. "Good God, the idiots."

"Ryan...please," she began in soothing tones, growing uncomfortable as the cynosure of the surrounding diners, but before she could continue, the waiter arrived at their table bearing a tray with their dinners.

She sat back while he placed the array of food on the table before them. Everything looked delicious. Everything smelled delicious. It made Lindsay feel slightly sick.

"Can I bring you another drink?" The waiter asked, glancing from one to the another.

"No, thank you," they answered in unison.

"Enjoy your dinner." The waiter departed.

"I don't know about you, but I'm famished," Ryan said, hungrily eyeing the thick cut of meat on his plate. "I suggest we continue our discussion after we've eaten."

Her appetite was completely gone, but there was no way Lindsay would admit that to him, not after he had, in effect, declared a peace of sorts...or at least a cessation of mutual verbal shots.

Lifting her fork, she speared a tiny corner of the fish and brought it to her lips. It was delicious, the delicate dill sauce enhancing the flavor. Another small bite and the sick feeling was vanquished, her appetite restored.

Determining to enjoy her meal, despite her irascible companion, she dredged up a smile, and cast about for some innocuous table conversation. "The fish is excellent. How is your steak?"

"Good." He popped another bite into his mouth, chewed methodically and swallowed before tacking on, "The potato and salad aren't bad, either." He slanted a droll, pointed look at her untouched side dishes. "The veggies are good for you, you know."

Lindsay had to laugh; he sounded so much like a chiding parent—like her when she chided either one or both of her daughters.

His mouth full of steak, he cocked that one eyebrow in a silent demand for an explanation for her amusement.

She smiled without restraint. "I'm sorry, but I

couldn't help myself. You sounded so like every scolding parent...like me, as a matter of fact."

He laughed, softly, easily.

Lindsay almost dropped her fork, nearly undone by the flood of warmth the sound of his rich masculine laughter infused inside her entire being.

Confused by the strong response to something so everyday and mundane as the sound of a man's laughter, Lindsay stared at him in bemusement for a moment.

"Go on, try the potato before it gets cold," he said, in obvious teasing, motioning with his fork at the foil-wrapped vegetable. "The salad will keep, it's already cold."

"All right, I give up," she surrendered, laughing again. "I'll taste the darned thing."

The meal progressed in relative congeniality.

"That's better," Ryan declared, after having devoured every morsel of his dinner. "I feel almost human again."

Her own meal greatly diminished, if not entirely consumed, Lindsay smiled and nodded in agreement.

"Dessert?" The waiter materialized at their table, as if conjured by the master magician of customer service. "An after-dinner drink?"

"No, thank you, nothing for me." Lindsay shook her head. "Ryan?"

He hesitated, then likewise shook his head. "No. Just the check, please."

Pondering his moment of indecision, Lindsay refrained from comment until after the waiter had left to fetch the check. "Ryan, if you wanted something else, dessert, a drink..." She broke off when he frowned and made a sharp, impatient move of his hand.

Her solicitousness rebuffed, Lindsay consigned the devil to the nether regions. She again felt sorely tempted, this time to insist on paying her share of the bill when it arrived, just because she felt certain her offer would annoy him.

The man was impossible, she fumed, preceding him from the restaurant. For Ashley's sake, she could only pray Logan wasn't as intractable as his father.

For herself, having been happily married to a gentle, soft-spoken, sensitive man, Lindsay couldn't imagine being married to any man, never mind such an obstinate, hardheaded tyrant as Ryan Callahan appeared to be.

But, Ashley was young, and had fallen in love, as her sister Mary had before her. Lindsay was happy for them, and wished for them nothing but continued happiness with the men whom, according to them, completed their lives.

Personally, she couldn't wait to get home to her cat.

She turned to face him, bid him good-night the minute they stepped outside the restaurant. He was so close behind her, she found herself staring at the base of his throat.

"I would have liked a cup of coffee," he said, drawing her startled gaze up to his watchful eyes. "I still would."

Lindsay stepped back, to ease the strain in her neck, she told herself, and most definitely not to distance herself from the warmth radiating from his body, the headiness of his scent teasing her senses.

"But..." she frowned in confusion. "If you wanted coffee, why didn't you order it?"

"If you'll recall," he began, then broke off to take her by the arm, move her with him to one side out of harm's way, as a chatting foursome exited the restaurant. "We agreed to suspend our discussion until after dinner."

A disquieting sensation sparked in Lindsay's stomach. "Yes...but..."

"Did you want to continue here," he cut in on her, "in the parking lot?"

"Of course not," she exclaimed. "But..."

"In one of our cars then?" he again cut in.

"No." She shook her head, the disquieting sensation intensifying. "But..."

"I was hoping you were planning to invite me back to your place." His voice again ran roughshod over hers. "And that you'd offer to make a pot of coffee."

Back to her place? The disquieting sensation expanded inside, robbing Lindsay of breath, of thought. Stunned by the very idea of him, all six feet two inches of him, in her home, of being alone with him there, drinking her coffee while he railed against his son and her daughter, sent a frisson of near panic skittering down her spine. Hell, the mere light touch of his large hand still curled around her arm was playing havoc with her nervous system.

"I...I..." Her stuttering attempt at speech betrayed her feelings of trepidation.

"You have nothing to fear from me, Lindsay," he drawled, his voice laced with humor. "I promise you, I will not lose my temper and attack…or even shout at you."

Lindsay felt like a fool, a hyper, naive teenager on her first date. This wasn't even a date, for pity's sake, she chastised herself. The man wanted to talk, that's all, discuss the reception she planned to arrange.

"I am not afraid of you, Ryan," she lied, lifting her chin to a haughty angle. "But it is late, and…"

"And it's not getting any earlier," he inserted, tugging on her arm to lead her toward the rows of parked vehicles. "So, what's it to be—yes or no?"

Lindsay wanted to say no, longed to say no, felt almost desperate to say no, but she could not, would not allow this, this intimidating man, to think—to know—how much he intimidated her.

She sighed…the sound of defeat.

He smiled…the sign of victory.

Lindsay's being was swept by an urge to slap the smile from his face which, coming so soon after the previous impulse, in itself was startling; she abhorred violence. Besides, she'd have had to jump up to reach his lean cheek. She returned his smile instead.

"All right," she said, yanking her arm from his loose hold. "Follow me, if you insist."

His only answer was a soft chuckle. It tickled her nape all the way home, every time she glanced in the rearview mirror to see his black Lincoln sedan looming behind her like some large and dark bird of prey.

Shrugging off the fanciful thought, Lindsay avoided the mirror and concentrated on the roadway.

As her assistant manager, Betty, had pointed out, the inn was not far from Lindsay's townhouse complex. She hit the remote before turning into her driveway. The garage door slid up, she drove inside, then sat for a moment, her gaze fixed to the car pulling into the driveway a moment later.

The garage door slid down. Lindsay sighed, for a second allowing herself the cowardly luxury of considering remaining where she was, hiding away from Ryan Callahan until he gave up and left. The only thing that got her moving, from the car into the house and through to the front door, was the absolute certainty that Ryan would not give up and leave.

She opened the door, stepped back, and invited him inside with a listless wave of her hand.

Ryan blessed her with laughing eyes and a knowing grin, revealing strong, incredibly white teeth.

Oh, sure, he would have perfect teeth, Lindsay thought irritably, irrelevantly, working her stiff lips into a parody of a welcoming smile.

"Have a seat," she said, already moving toward the kitchen, away from his overpowering presence.

"Would you mind if I have a look around?"

Lindsay paused midflight to glance back at him. That one dratted eyebrow was arched, only this time it didn't convey mockery or derision, but blatant wicked deviltry.

How did he manage that subtle change in expression simply by the raising of the same eyebrow? she asked herself, suppressing a reflexive shiver of... something.

"Be my guest," she responded, flippantly, covering a reluctance to him examining, judging her so carefully chosen pieces of furniture and decorative objects.

"I thought I was," he rejoined, unconcealed amusement coloring his soft tones.

Frustrated by his obvious penchant for having the last word, Lindsay stormed into the kitchen. Working with her normal smooth and efficient movements, she set about preparing coffee, decaf, all the while telling herself she had to be out of her mind to have allowed him to maneuver her into this uncomfortable situation.

The slight rattle of cups against saucers brought him like a homing pigeon to the kitchen doorway.

"Smells good." Leaning against the smooth oak door frame, he sent a casual-looking glance around the room.

Watching him, Lindsay felt positive his seemingly cursory inspection didn't miss a thing, that he noted, in detail, the sheen on the fitted oak cabinets above and below the textured white countertop, the matching oak of the table surface and chair legs, the satin finish of the stainless steel appliances and sink, the lacy ecru curtains, the muted green-and-cranberry wallpaper, the pristine white floor tiles swirled through with random curls of the same muted green and cranberry, down to the black-and-steel coffeemaker when his roving gaze came to a halt, on her.

"You have a nice place here," he said, his voice low, somehow disturbing. "Comfortable and homey. Did you decorate it yourself?"

"Yes."

He nodded, as if to say he'd expected as much. "You did a good job."

"Thank you." As compliments went, his wasn't the most lavish she had ever heard, and yet, inexplicably, it pleased her more than other raves she had received for her efforts.

He smiled, a faint, slow, impossibly sensuous smile and sauntered into the spacious room, diminishing it by his tall imposing form.

Suddenly feeling crowded, almost stalked, Lindsay remained stock-still, her breathing shallow, her nerves twanging, her mind a blank space between her ears.

"May I?" Ryan indicated a padded, armed dinette chair neatly placed at the round table.

Lindsay snapped out of her frozen rabbit state. "Yes, of course, the...uh, coffee will be ready in a minute. And I've set some cookies out," she nodded to the plate in the center of the table. She was babbling, she knew she was babbling, she just couldn't seem to stop. "Do you take cream, sugar?" She sidled around the opposite side of the table to go to the fridge.

His gaze steady on her, he circled the table, coming to a stop less than two feet from her in front of the large double-door appliance.

Lindsay's throat and mouth went bone-dry. Without thought, she wet her lips. Ryan's gaze dropped to her mouth. A flare lit the depths of his eyes, now more emerald green than hazel. Her heart rate increased. For an instant, she stood frozen, staring at the curve of his sculpted lips. Anticipatory moisture rushed to her throat, her mouth.

He slowly lowered his head. That close, she could see the lines fanning his eyes—squint lines, or laugh lines? Lindsay wondered in vague fascination. Probably not laugh lines, she mused, growing weak as he drew closer.

She closed her eyes.

His breath misted her lips.

At that moment, a ball of fur launched itself from the top of the fridge onto Ryan's left shoulder and curled its sinuous body around his neck.

"What the hell," he barked, jerking back.

Startled by his abrupt movement, the cat emitted a high-pitched yowl and, extending its claws, flailed its paws for purchase.

"*Sheba,*" Lindsay exclaimed, shocked and mortified by her pet's strange behavior.

Rushing forward, she reached out and grasped the cat, tugging its claws free of Ryan's jacket before plucking it from its perch around his neck. "Oh, Ryan, I'm so sorry." Her eyes widened as she noticed the claw tears in his suit coat. "Oh, Lord, look at your jacket!"

He barely spared a glance for the slashes on his shoulder inflicted by the cat's rear paws. "An attack cat?" he muttered, staring at her in disbelief. "You have an attack cat?"

"Sheba's not an attack cat," Lindsay said in defense of the wriggling feline clutched in the crook of her arm. "She has never done anything like this before."

His expression skeptical, Ryan eyed the fluffy-haired white cat with wary censure.

Lindsay opened her mouth to repeat her assertion, and her apology, but her gaze brushed his shoulder, flickering at the tears in the material, before moving on, and the only sound to emerge from her throat

RYAN OBJECTS

138

was an appalled gasp at the sight of the trickle of blood seeping from two scratches on the side of his neck, staining the collar of his white shirt.

She dropped the cat to raise a hand to her mouth.

Sheba screeched in protest.

"What?" Ryan demanded, casting the cat an annihilating look as it proceeded to coil itself around his ankles.

"Ohmygosh..." she cried. "You're *bleeding*."

Chapter Three

Some days it just didn't pay to get out of bed.

Wincing as he dabbed antiseptic onto the shallow scratches on his neck, Ryan's thoughts continued along the same path, cataloging the day's events.

To begin, even after twelve hours of dead-to-the-world sleep, he'd awakened still feeling beat, not quite with it, and late for work.

His mind foggy with jet lag, his stomach grumbling from hunger, Ryan had showered, dressed and left his apartment, stopping at a local coffee shop for a decent breakfast before going on to his office.

Which was why he hadn't played back the messages on his home answering machine.

Which was why he had first heard the news about his son's spur-of-the-moment elopement via his office machine, from Logan's brand-new mother-in-law, Lindsay Dawson.

Feeling a resurgence of the anger that had roared

through him on hearing the woman rattle on about making plans for a delayed wedding reception for the *happy* couple, Ryan sighed as he applied antibiotic cream to the two wounds and followed it up with two bandages.

Controlling the roiling anger enough to concentrate on the mound of paperwork that had accumulated during his extended business trip to Japan hadn't been easy. In fact it had been damned difficult when what he wanted to do was take off to visit the woman and tell her what she could do with her gushy-voiced idea.

Logan's call sometime later, with his excuse of "I fell in love" for his precipitous action, hadn't gone very far in alleviating Ryan's disgruntlement.

And working through lunch had merely ascerbated his irritation so that by the time he'd driven to King of Prussia to confront Logan's mother-in-law, rather than having calmed down, Ryan's anger still simmered on a high burner.

Yeah, it would have been much better if he had simply stayed in bed that morning, Ryan's ring-around-the-rosie ruminations all fell down exactly where they had started.

If he had stayed in bed, he wouldn't now be doctoring cat claw scratches on his neck, little almost nothing scratches that had so upset Lindsay.

"Do you think you should have a shot?" she'd asked with anxious concern.

"Of scotch?" he'd retorted.

"No." She'd given him an impatient, agitated look. "You know what I mean."

"Are you afraid your cat might have rabies?"

He'd been teasing, attempting to calm her down. His question only seemed to agitate her more.

"Of course not," she'd yelped, as if stung. "Sheba's had all her shots."

"So have I," he'd assured her.

She'd moved to him, her soft bottom lip caught between her teeth. "Come with me to the bathroom. I'll clean it and see if you should see a doctor."

That had done it; Ryan hated visiting a doctor, even for his once yearly checkups. He had beat a hasty retreat, avoiding her insistence of fussing over him.

Ryan hated anyone fussing over him even more than he hated visiting a doctor. And, although he had always liked animals—Logan had had a cat when he was young—at that precise moment, he had hated that feline.

By the same token, if he had stayed in bed that morning, he wouldn't have as yet met the woman with the excited, kinda giddy, kinda sultry, strangely arousing voice.

Lindsay.

Lindsay of the teeth-melting smile.

Ryan groaned, and stared in bemusement at his reflection in the bathroom mirror.

He had come to within an inch of kissing the tempting mouth forming her smile.

Who could explain physical attraction? Ryan silently asked his somber reflection in the mirror. When he had left his office late that afternoon, he'd had every intention of setting her straight about his feelings concerning her idea of a delayed reception, then proceeding on to the award dinner.

And yet, a few short hours later, he had found himself facing her in her kitchen, drawn almost—well almost, but not quite—against his will to the magnetic pull of her attractions, the softly round curves of her small body, the allure of her gentle dark eyes, the temptation of her full, slightly parted lips.

And he had almost touched those lips with his own, tasted their promise of sweetness.

Damn cat.

A chuckle rumbled in Ryan's throat, and he shook his head at his own image, and arousing imaginings, before turning to exit the room.

That ball of pure white fur sure put a quick end to his amorous intentions, and he knew it was pure white, he had the hairs clinging to his left pant leg to prove it, he reflected, dropping naked onto the bed.

So, of course, they never had gotten around to discussing her blasted plan to throw a belated reception for the impulsive couple of idiots.

Yawning, Ryan settled into a comfortable position, flinging one arm over his head. Sleep teasing the edges of his mind, a final thought filtered through his fuzzy brain before slumber swept him away.

He would have to meet with her again.

Ryan fell asleep with a satisfied smile on his lips.

Lindsay woke to Sheba perched on her hip, mewling in her ear for her breakfast.

"Oh, go away," she muttered, dislodging her pet with a gentle sweep of her arm. Ignoring the cat's indignant yowl, she buried her face deeper into her pillow.

Lindsay had spent a long, restless night, fraught

with anxiety over the damage inflicted on Ryan by her pet. She didn't even know how deep a trough the animal's claws had made on the side of his neck, as Ryan had refused to allow her to examine the wounds. Telling her he'd take care of it himself, he had beat a hasty retreat...after shaking the coiling feline off of his left leg.

The alarm rang. Groaning, Lindsay grouped for the bedside table and fumbled to depress the Off button. Sheba leaped back onto her hip, her mournful demand for food more effective than the alarm in extricating Lindsay from beneath the bedcovers.

"Wicked creature," she scolded, stumbling to the bathroom. "You can just wait until after I've had my shower." She cast the cat dogging her footsteps a glowering look. "And if you follow me in here," she said in warning, "I'll turn the shower spray on you."

As if she understood every word, Sheba raised her elegant head, and her long fluffy tail, leveled a haughty, amber-eyed look at her mistress, and strolled away.

Fifteen minutes later, showered and dressed for work, Lindsay entered the kitchen. Only then did she deign to fill the cat's empty food bowl.

With Sheba daintily nibbling at her breakfast, Lindsay went to the coffeemaker. Sighing, she dumped the liner of limp, damp grounds and then the carafe of cold coffee she had made for Ryan, and had gone untouched.

What must he be thinking? The question had tormented Lindsay at odd, wakeful moments throughout the seemingly endless night. For the life of her, she couldn't imagine what had gotten into Sheba; her pet had never done anything like that before, as she had tried, several times, to assure Ryan. He had merely given the cat a wary look, attempting to shake her off his leg while making a beeline for the front door.

The whole episode had been worse than a bad romantic comedy movie scenario, she thought, wincing as she dropped a piece of seven grain bread into the toaster.

Still, the aftereffects of the fiasco, upsetting as they were, were not the primary cause of her restless night. The biggest agent of torment resided with the absolute certainty that Ryan had been on the point of kissing her when Sheba decided to do a nosedive off the refrigerator.

Slanting a baleful glance at the innocent-appearing feline slowly making inroads into her food, Lindsay poured herself a cup of coffee and plucked the bread from the toaster. Buttering the toast, and collecting milk from the fridge, she settled at the table. Absently munching a bite of toast, she stared into middle distance.

What would his kiss be like? *That* was the question that had really played havoc with her slumber.

But she hadn't wanted him to kiss her... Had she? She didn't want him to kiss her... Did she?

An image formed in her mind of Ryan's beautifully sculpted, masculine mouth, drawing closer, closer to her own, the tantalizing warmth of his breath feathering her lips.

A tiny shiver slithered down Lindsay's spine. Her breathing grew shallow, her pulse pounded, her...

"*Sheba,*" Lindsay yelped, when the cat jumped

into her lap and curled into a purring ball. "Get down at once," she ordered, shooing the animal away. "Look what you've done. You've got hair all over my skirt," she grumbled, brushing at the deposit of white fur.

Unfazed by Lindsay's harangue, Sheba tossed her head, regally paced to the basket bed in the corner, curled up on the plump cushion, and promptly fell asleep.

She had spoiled the cat rotten, Lindsay remonstrated with herself, finishing her coffee and taking the cup and her bread plate to the sink. Came from being alone too much, she supposed. But one did get lonely with too many hours spent alone, too few visits from family.

Lindsay's immediate family consisted of two daughters, Ashley, the oldest, and Mary, the baby.

Lindsay smiled; Mary was far from a baby anymore. She was the first of the girls to marry—and a lavish, if hectic, affair it had been, too. Lindsay had suffered near exhaustion to prove it. Mary now quite efficiently managed the original Lindsay's Intimates store Lindsay had opened soon after her husband's untimely death.

Although Ashley had helped out in the store throughout her teenage years, and still did if needed at the busiest times of the year, she had little enthusiasm for the business, preferring her position of office manager and sometime medical assistant at the Flatrock Medical Center, located outside Allentown, the family's home city.

Before deciding to branch out and open another store in King of Prussia, Lindsay had never been lonely...well, at any rate, at least not too often. But after opening the new store, she had soon tired of making the sixty-odd-mile trip every day, and had relocated, buying the townhouse a mere fifteen minutes from the large complex comprising The Court and The Plaza malls.

Within months, with too much time on her hands, even with the long hours she had put in at the store, loneliness had set in. Lindsay had bought Sheba for company.

And now, that arrogant feline had chased away the one and only male Lindsay had ever invited back to her home.

Not that she wanted or desired a male in her home, or her life after all these years, Lindsay assured herself. She had had one near relationship with a man a couple of years after Jeffrey's death, a contemporary of her husband's, in fact. But, although she had liked him, very much, something inside her had cringed when he had tried to deepen their relationship from one of friendship to a more intimate, physical level.

Other than the occasional evening out, for dinner, the theater, she had not formed an association with any man since that time, now some fifteen years ago.

Nevertheless, by dint of Ashley and Logan's sudden decision to marry, Ryan Callahan had been made, however unwillingly, a part of her life.

And, Lindsay further concluded, she should contact him to again apologize for her pet's strange behavior—she shot the sleeping cat a frustrated look—and ask how he was feeling this morning. Besides, despite the strained situation last night, she still thought it best to solicit his opinion and preferences concerning the delayed wedding reception.

Glancing at the range-top clock, Lindsay calculated she had enough time before she had to leave to open the store for a quick call to his office. If Ryan wasn't yet in his office, she'd leave a message, as she had before, she decided, grabbing the Post-it note with his business and home phone numbers from the side of the fridge.

Refilling her coffee cup, Lindsay carried it, the note and the portable phone to the table. The phone rang, startling her, before she had settled in a chair.

Telepathy? she wondered, somehow certain the caller was Ryan. But it wasn't; it was her daughter.

"Morning, Mom," Mary said, sounding wide awake and ready to take on the world. "I know you're probably just about ready to leave for the store. So am I. But I thought I'd give you a quick call to find out if you had managed to contact Logan's father yet about your plan for a reception."

What to answer? *Yes, I've contacted him and the man is impossible to pin down?* Lindsay shook her head, knowing an ambiguous answer like that would only elicit more questions from Mary. So, in the ageless, tried-and-true mother fashion, she employed delaying tactics.

"Yes...well, actually, I left a message on his office answering machine and Mr. Callahan contacted me," she admitted. "But it was late in the day...and we really didn't get to a meaningful discussion on the matter," she qualified. "In fact, I was just about to give him a call to arrange a meeting with him."

"Oh, fine, then I'll let you go. Have you heard anything more from Ashley?"

"No, dear, but then, I didn't expect to," Lindsay said. "Ashley and Logan are on their honeymoon, you know," she chided. "And I don't recall hearing from you when you were on your honeymoon."

"Point taken." Mary laughed. "Talk to you later. "I'm off to open the store. Bye."

Smiling and shaking her head, Lindsay pressed the Disconnect button and glanced at the clock. Deciding she could still spare a few minutes, she punched in Ryan's office number.

His secretary was brisk but polite, and asked Lindsay to "Hold, please."

Sighing, she began to tap one fingernail on the tabletop, but within three taps, Ryan picked up.

"Callahan."

"Is that how you always answer your phone?" Lindsay asked, frowning at his abrupt response.

"Yes," he answered, in tones not at all apologetic. "What can I do for you, Lindsay?"

She felt a flash of impatient irritation at his tone and his obtuseness. Didn't he know? "I would think that would be obvious," she returned, using considerable restraint to keep her own tones pleasant. "I called to ask how you were feeling this morning."

"I could say with my hands," he rejoined, a thread of humor fraying his clipped tones. "But I won't...wouldn't want to date myself."

She sighed again, noisily this time. "I was referring to your wounds," she said, repressively.

"Which ones?" Ryan retorted. "The wounds to my neck, or the ones to my dignity?"

"Your neck, of course," she shot back, thoroughly annoyed. "As I didn't know you had any dignity."

He laughed.

Lindsay's lips twitched. Darn the man...and the attractive sound of his laughter. "Now that you've had your fun, will you tell me how you're feeling?"

"I'm fine, Lindsay." His voice had changed, lowered, softened; she almost wished it hadn't...soft and low, it was far too appealing.

"But the scratches..." she began.

"Were just scratches," he inserted. "Not deep, not dangerous, mere scratches."

"Well, that's a relief." Lindsay paused, not sure how to broach the subject of the wedding reception, considering his reluctance to discuss it last night. Ryan made it easy for her by bringing it up himself.

"You know, thanks to your attack cat, we never did get around to our discussion...and I didn't get the cup of coffee I wanted, either."

Sure, lay a guilt trip on me, why don't you? Lindsay thought, as if she already didn't feel terrible enough about the unfortunate incident, and having stonewalled Mary. "Sheba is not an attack cat," she protested, heatedly.

"Sheba," he repeated, as if musing on the name. "Rather exotic name for a house cat, isn't it?"

"Well, perhaps," she conceded. "But it seems to fit her, as I'm convinced she believes she's a queen."

"Hmm...the warrior kind," he murmured.

"She is not an attack cat," she insisted.

"So you said, several times," he drawled. "I'm reserving judgment on the beast."

Lindsay ground her teeth, positive she knew ex-

actly who the beast was in this instance. Still, she
had to deal with this particular beast, she reminded
herself; he was now a member of the family, if only
by marriage.

And, she reminded herself, she'd never get to the
subject of the primary order of business by arguing
with him about her pet. "Suit yourself," she said,
letting her growing impatience show. "But could we
please get back to our interrupted discussion?"

"You owe me a cup of coffee."

Lindsay blinked, then had to laugh. It was either
laugh or scream. The man could try the patience of
a saint.

"But I'll buy," Ryan continued after a slight
pause. "If you'll agree to have dinner with me again
tonight."

Lindsay frowned. Dinner with him? In a restaurant? She had a memory flash of last night, and the
covert glances from the other patrons when she had
attempted to discuss the reception with Ryan.

No way, was her first thought. But, she did need
to meet with him, finally make some headway regarding the reception. If not in a restaurant, where?

"I promise I'll behave," he said into her conster-
nated silence.

Oh, sure, like a ranting wild man, she thought.
Darn it, if he didn't want any part in planning a reception—for his son, as well as her daughter—why
didn't he just say so, instead of playing the heavy-
handed parent? Getting no answers to her own questions, Lindsay raked her mind for a solution, and
blurted out the first one to pop into her head.

"We could have dinner here," she said, asking

herself if she had lost her mind, while at the same time feeling a tingle of anticipation. "Since I owe you a cup of coffee," she tacked on as an excuse for her moment of seeming insanity, and ignoring the tingle.

"With the cat?" Ryan asked with gentle sarcasm.

No doubt about it, she had lost her mind, she berated herself. "I'll make a deal with you," she said, returning his sarcasm drenched with self-impatience. "I'll promise you that Sheba will behave, if you'll stick to your promise to do likewise. A deal?"

"You're going to cook, or order in?"

"I'll cook." Had he thought she couldn't?

"It's a deal." He laughed.

She really wished he wouldn't do that. "Good." Wrong, she corrected herself, wondering how and why she had opened her mouth and put herself in this position. There wasn't a darned thing good about it.

"What time, and what can I bring?" he asked, amusement still dancing on his voice...and her senses.

"Seven?"

"Fine. And...?"

"Wine," she said, for want of a better idea.

"White or red?"

Oh, Lord, the man was a human battering ram. What could she prepare? Lindsay scoured her mind, and grasped at an idea. Something with red meat. The beast liked red meat.

"Red," she said.

"Any particular type?"

Oh, save me, she pleaded in silent desperation. She rolled her eyes. "You choose."

"Okay. See you at seven." He hung up on her.

"Well, goodbye to you, too," she said, casting a sour look at the phone and disconnecting.

Exhausted, Lindsay slumped against the chair back, feeling as if she had gone twelve rounds with the heavyweight champion of the world.

Now all she had to do was figure out what to cook for her opponent. She couldn't broil a couple of steaks, Lindsay reminded herself; Ryan had had steak last night. And there wouldn't be enough time after she got home from work to prepare a roast...

Work.

Good heavens, while sparring with Ryan, she'd lost sight of the time, she chided herself. Jumping up, she carried her cup to the sink, rinsed it, then ran upstairs to the bathroom to brush her teeth and hair. If she didn't get moving, she'd be late to open the store.

Deep in cat slumber, Sheba didn't so much as flick the tip of her tail at Lindsay's mad dash around the house, collecting her purse and keys before rushing out the door into the garage and jumping into her car.

"Meat loaf!" Lindsay exclaimed, laughing as she backed her car out of the garage. To her memory, she couldn't think of one man she knew who didn't love meat loaf.

It was six-thirty. Everything was ready. The meat loaf was baking in the oven, alongside a casserole dish of cheddar cheese potatoes. A bowl of spinach

salad was chilling in the fridge. The table in the small
dining room alcove, which was seldom used, was set.

Lindsay was a good cook, and she knew it. Yet
she felt apprehensive. Her face felt flushed. Her
palms were moist. Giving the food in the oven, and
then the table, a final critical check, she headed for
the bathroom for a quick shower.

As Lindsay had hoped, Sheba padded behind her.
After a jump-in, sluice down, jump-out shower,
then a quick application of makeup, she dashed into
the bedroom to dress, Sheba at her heels.

What to wear? What to wear? Lindsay wasted precious minutes riffling through her closet before, exasperated with herself, she grabbed a pair of black
silk, wide-legged pants and a white silk, long-sleeved
overblouse.

By the time she had finished dressing and slipped
into soft, black leather flats, Sheba was curled up in
the middle of the bed, sound asleep, just as Lindsay
had hoped.

Tiptoeing from the room, she carefully closed the
door, shutting the cat inside, away from Ryan.

Returning to the kitchen, Lindsay glanced at the
clock. It was six minutes to seven. Hoping Ryan
would be punctual, she began slicing a long loaf of
crusty bread she had picked up at the market, along
with every other component of the meal, including
dessert.

Fortunately—or unfortunately depending on one's
point of view at the time—business in the store was
a little slow that day. Lindsay had left earlier than
usual to give herself plenty of time to shop and prepare the meal.

Now, with everything ready, Ryan due to arrive
any moment, and her stomach busy tying itself into
knots, Lindsay wasn't sure if she'd be able to eat a
bite.

Chapter Four

Ryan felt a mite edgy. A little apprehensive. A tiny bit nervous. And not one of those feelings had a thing to do with Sheba, the queen of attack cats.

He could handle Sheba. What Ryan didn't know was if he could handle Lindsay. And he wanted to handle her. Man, how he wanted to handle her. He wanted to handle her in the time-honored ways a man handles a woman he's interested in, fascinated by, sexually attracted to.

But Lindsay was so small, so delicate, so fragile-looking…and so damned tempting.

Lord, had it really only been one day since he first laid eyes on her? Ryan marveled, neatly making the turn into her driveway. Strange, but it seemed like he had known her, or been waiting to know her, forever.

That wasn't strange, he corrected himself, setting the hand break. That was bizarre, fantasy stuff.

Ryan sat still for a moment, contemplating on his hands gripping the wheel, the slight tremor in his fingers, the feeling of anticipation shimmering inside him.

A frown pulled his dark eyebrows together. Hell, he hadn't felt this wound up about a woman since... Ryan's frown deepened. So far as he could recollect, he had *never* felt quite this wound up, complexity of emotions, about a woman.

Ryan's frown grew into a fierce scowl. He was forty-seven years old, for Pete's sake. He was past the age, well past, of going around the bend over a female.

Maybe he was having a midlife crisis, no doubt brought on by his son's headlong leap into matrimony.

Naw. Ryan shook his head. He was much too hardheaded to succumb to a biological urge to cut loose, take to wearing his shirt unbuttoned to mid-chest and drape gold chains around his neck. Besides, he was too big to cram himself into the requisite low-slung racy-looking sports car, he thought, a smile teasing his lips.

Chuckling at his own ridiculous mental meanderings, Ryan glanced at the dashboard clock. It read 6:55. Perfect. Right on time.

Grabbing the neck of the still-cold bottle of California cabernet he had removed from the wine rack in his refrigerator, Ryan stepped from the car and loped along the flagstone walkway to the front door.

He raised a hand, finger poised to ring the door-bell, and paused to draw a deep breath.

Lindsay was inside, waiting for him, expecting

him to kick up difficult, give her a hard time about her idea to plan a reception for Logan and Ashley.

In truth, with the passage of a day and a half to get used to the idea, Ryan had faced the fact that at twenty-seven, his son was long past the age of needing his father's permission for anything, most especially who or when he should marry.

So, that being the case, Ryan thought, why not throw a party for the idiotic newlyweds?

Deciding to tell Lindsay at once, Ryan again moved his finger toward the bell, and again hesitated when a devious idea slithered into his mind.

On second thought, sparring with Lindsay was loads of fun and extremely exciting. So far, as Ryan had been able to discern, he had not managed to intimidate her in the least. Quite the opposite. He had merely riled her. And when Lindsay was riled, her softly curved delectable form quivered, her eyes sparkled with challenge, and her tantalizing tongue lashed with honey-tipped abandon.

The anticipation shimmering inside Ryan expanded into a sizzling crackle. Given the opportunity, he'd capture and trap her sweet tongue inside his mouth.

Smiling, his nefarious course set, Ryan at last pressed his finger to the doorbell. A moment later, the door swung open and Lindsay was standing there, looking good enough to ravish in clingy silk black pants and white shirt.

"You're very punctual," she said, stepping back and motioning him inside. "It's exactly seven."

"I'm also starving." He smiled as he moved by her, inhaling the intoxicating mouthwatering aromas of cooking food and her senses-stirring scent. "The wine is chilled." He handed her the bottle. "Dinner about ready?"

She laughed; the sound of it did a shivery shimmy the length of his spine. "Yes, it's ready," she said, skirting around him and heading for the kitchen. "All I have to do is set it out. The powder room's here, if you want to wash up." She tapped a closed door as she walked past.

Ryan stood still for an instant, tormenting his libido by watching the gentle sway of her hips. Then, coming to his senses, he scanned a look around the room. "Where's the warrior queen of the attack cats?" he called after her.

She halted in the kitchen doorway to toss a wry look back at him over her shoulder. "Afraid to move, Ryan? You needn't be," she continued on before he could respond. "She's shut up inside my bedroom."

Lucky cat. Banishing the lascivious thoughts spawned by the contemplation of being shut up with Lindsay in her bedroom that rushed into his mind, Ryan stepped into the minuscule powder room, washed his hands and smoothed back the unruly lock of hair that persisted in falling onto his forehead. When he stepped out again, all he had to do was follow his nose, his stomach making a low sound of appreciation for the smell he hoped he had correctly identified.

"We'll eat in the dining room," Lindsay said, indicating the small alcove off one side of the kitchen. "I hope you like meat loaf."

"I love meat loaf," Ryan told her, his hope fulfilled. "Anything I can do to help?"

"Yes, you can open the wine and bring it and that basket of bread on the counter to the table."

Ryan performed the simple task and followed her into the small alcove. He liked it, that near-tiny room. It was intimate, conducive to quiet conversation, definitely not contentious bickering, however exciting and enjoyable he found their clashes to be.

At his suggestion, they again put off the discussion of the reception until after they had finished eating. Ryan had a hard time suppressing a smile at Lindsay's sigh of relief.

The meal far surpassed the expectations instilled in him by the cooking aromas. Though Ryan employed a service to clean his condo once a week, he had never hired a cook, preferring to use his own limited culinary skills or eat out. It had been ages since he had enjoyed a home-cooked meal, never mind a superior one, and he savored every bite.

"You're some mean cook," he complimented Lindsay, accepting her offer of another slice of meat loaf, his third. "This is the best meat loaf I've ever tasted." He raised his glass in a silent salute to her.

"Thank you." She smiled. His teeth melted...into the meat. "It's my mother's recipe."

"The rest ain't bad, either," he said in teasing.

"The potatoes are from a box."

He shook his head, finished chewing, and said, "I don't care."

She smiled again. This time his bones melted. "So is the dessert...well, a box from the freezer."

"What kind?"

Her eyes grew bright; his knees went weak.

"Oh, you know," she said with mock seriousness. "The run-of-the-mill square box."

Ryan compressed his lips against a smile, and gave her what he hoped was a droll look.

She laughed; he went weak all over.

"I hope you like it." Her laughter, and the brightness in her eyes faded. "It's New York–style cheesecake."

"I like it," he was quick to assure her, willing to risk his teeth and his nervous system to see her smile again.

"That's a relief." Sliding her chair back, she moved to rise. "I'll go start the coffee and cut the cake while you finish eating."

His mouth full of the last of the meat on his plate, Ryan gave a quick, hard shake of his head to keep her seated. She frowned. He swallowed. "I'm stuffed, couldn't handle dessert right away. And the coffee can wait." Picking up the bottle, he topped off her glass, then his own. "We can talk while we finish our wine."

For a second, conflicting expressions of relief and apprehension flickered over her face, in her eyes, leaving little doubt in Ryan's mind that she expected him to launch into a rant against their respective offspring.

"You can relax, Lindsay," he said, smiling to relieve her anxiety. "I promised I'd behave."

"And do you keep your promises?" she asked, uncertainty shading her soft voice.

"Yes," he answered in a firm, unequivocal tone.

"Okay." She settled back in her chair, obviously expecting him to finally discuss the reception.

"Wait a minute, I've got a better idea," he said, sliding his chair back. "Let's clear away the dishes, then go into the living room, where we can talk in comfort."

Lindsay hesitated a moment, before nodding agreement. "All right," she said, rising. "I'll also start the coffee, that way it'll be ready when we are."

Working together with mutual smooth efficiency, they made quick work of the chore. Ryan was not surprised, pleased but not surprised. He had a gut feeling certainty they would be good together at many things. That pleased him even more.

Lindsay poured water into the coffeemaker, then stood staring at her trembling fingers. The betraying tremor had started when Ryan brushed her arm while moving from the dining room to the kitchen, carting dishes to her while she loaded the dishwasher.

Though Lindsay had chided herself for the silly reaction to the brief touch of his arm against hers, it hadn't helped; the tremor persisted, along with a warm, squishy sensation that coursed through the length of her body,

The combined surface and inner sensations had so disturbed her, Lindsay had shooed him from the room with the nearly empty wine bottle and their glasses, telling him that she'd join him in a few minutes, and to make himself comfortable.

One of them may as well be comfortable, Lindsay mused, and it might as well be Ryan, because she most assuredly was not in the least comfortable.

Silly, indeed. Lindsay frowned, confused by her so unusual reaction to Ryan. What was it about him, this particular man that caused this shimmery nervousness, this breathless sense of expectancy? Though undeniably Ryan was an attractive man, in every sense of the word, she had known, still knew, many attractive men, and yet she had never reacted to any one of them in such a strong, almost compelling way.

Truth be told, not even her husband Jeffrey had had such an intense effect on her from the moment they met. She had felt attracted to Jeffrey, interested in him, but strangely not to the physical and emotional degree she had been experiencing since Ryan had first commanded her attention.

Lindsay sighed and sent a trepid glance at the kitchen doorway. She was stalling, and she knew it. She also knew, with intuitive certainty, that if she didn't join him in the living room, and soon, he'd come looking for her.

Dismayed and excited at one and the same time by the certainty, Lindsay drew a deep, fortifying breath and propelled herself away from the countertop and to the doorway.

The first thing Lindsay noticed about him upon entering the room was that he was seated on the sofa, nearly reclining, his long legs stretched out in front of him, ankles crossed. His arms were draped, elbows propped on the low back of the sofa, their wineglasses casually cupped in each hand, presenting a picture of relaxed elegance.

Ryan had removed his suit jacket and tie, revealing the true width and breadth of his shoulders and chest. Worse still, he had opened his collar and cuff buttons, and had rolled his sleeves up. His forearms and the back of his fingers were shaded by a sprinkling of fine dark hairs. Lindsay was struck by a flashing speculation of whether his chest beneath his shirt was sprinkled with fine dark hairs, as well, or if it was matted by a thick diamond-shaped whorl, tapering to a trail down his muscular torso.

Appalled by the trend of her thoughts, the tightening tension inside her, Lindsay headed for the prim-looking Queen Anne chair opposite the sofa.

"Come, sit here next to me," Ryan ordered, if in an enticing murmur.

She hesitated.

Ryan raised that one eyebrow in a challenging arch.

Amazing, Lindsay thought, how he could convey so much with just the movement of that one darned eyebrow. Still, she stood there, uncertain and hesitant.

He chuckled.

Stung, she caved.

Struggling to appear as relaxed and casual as he looked, she shrugged and moved to the sofa to sit down...in the corner farthest from him.

"So, tell me about yourself," Ryan said in an amused drawl as soon as she had settled into the corner.

Lindsay blinked in confusion, startled by his verbal curveball. "What?"

"You," he said, handing a glass to her. "I want to hear about you, your life...and loves."

She grabbed the glass like a lifeline, and took several, very unladylike gulps. "Wh...why? I...er, mean...what does my life—" she shied away from the word *loves* ''—have to do with...er, the reception?'' Lindsay sputtered, raising her glass for deeper gulp, almost draining it.

Smiling, Ryan leaned to her, plucked the glass from her hand, and set it and his own glass on a table at his end of the sofa. ''I don't want you smashed, Lindsay,'' he said, ''Just mellow enough to talk to me about yourself.''

''But...'' She broke off to swallow, wondering how her throat could be so dry after all that wine. ''I thought we were going to discuss the wedding reception.''

Ryan sighed, impatience flickering across his expression, in his eyes. ''Bump the damned reception,'' he said with harsh abruptness. ''I'm trying to tell you I'm interested in you...you personally, Lindsay, not some stupid party for our flaky, lamebrained impetuous kids.''

For a moment, Lindsay just stared at him, struck mute by emotional conflicts consisting of being taken aback by his outburst, inordinately flattered by his admission of interest in her, and a surge of anger over his insulting reference to the character of their children, most especially *her* daughter. When she recovered her voice, she let it flay him.

''I can't speak for your son, Mr. Callahan,'' she snapped. ''But my daughter is not flaky, lamebrained or impetuous. Ashley is an intelligent, levelheaded young woman.''

''Oh, of course,'' he retorted, sliding over the seat cushions to within a foot of her. ''Every intelligent, levelheaded young person rushes headfirst into a quicky marriage after a weeklong acquaintance.''

"You did," she retaliated. "You admitted as much."

"I knew Logan's mother longer than a week," he shot back at her. "And I still paid a high price for what was, in truth, common, ordinary lust."

"But Ashley and Logan are not you and his mother," Lindsay cried in protest against his inference of lust being the driving force behind the couple's actions. "Hasn't it occurred to you that they just might be genuinely in love?"

"Actually, no," he said with biting candor. "What did occur to me was that the physical attraction between them was so immediate and strong, they divorced common sense to get married to indulge in it."

"Sex isn't everything," Lindsay protested heatedly. Incensed, she drew a deep breath...and felt a quaking inner shiver when his gaze dropped to her heaving breasts.

"Maybe not, but it's a lot." Ryan raised his gaze to hers, stealing her breath with the smoldering desire darkening his hazel eyes to pure green. "And for me, right now, this minute, it's a whole hell of a lot."

And suddenly, for Lindsay—the woman who had not been tempted into intimacy by any man since her husband—right then, that minute, it was a whole hell of a lot, too.

It was ridiculous, unthinkable. And yet, ridiculous or not, she could think of little else but being as one with this man she barely knew. Madness.

Her mind rattled by the self-knowledge, clouded by the flash fire of desire burning inside her, Lindsay stared at him, the inner flames leaping as he moved closer, closer.

"I'm going to kiss you." His voice was low, raspy with need, exciting in the extreme.

"Ryan." Her voice was little more than a burned cinder of a whisper.

His mouth brushed hers.

Lindsay shivered.

She moaned, softly, deep in her throat.

"Ah, Lindsay," he murmured, pulling her into his arms and taking thrilling command of her mouth with his own.

His chest was hard against her breasts, crushing them, arousing the budding tips. His lips slanted over hers, coaxing them apart. His tongue tested her inner sweetness, then drove deep to savor the honey.

Sighing, Lindsay went soft against him, surrendering to the pleasure of delights rippling through her from the singeing possession of his mouth, the tingling heaviness of her breasts, the melting warmth in her feminine core.

It was sheer heaven, but she wanted more. Curling her arms around his neck, she arched into him in a silent, telling demand for closer contact.

Ryan responded with satisfying swiftness. Gliding his hand down her back to her thighs, he swept her legs up, onto the sofa, then covered her body with his own, making her aware of the extent of his arousal.

It, he, felt wonderful...and scary. Needing to breathe, and possibly even think, Lindsay broke the kiss by turning her head to face the back of the sofa. Ryan took advantage, and her quick breath, by exploring the curve of her exposed neck with his lips and tongue.

This had to stop, she thought, fuzzily, before she, he, did something foolish. "Ryan, the coffee's done," she blurted out inanely. "And we didn't have dessert."

"You're so hot, and so sweet," he murmured against her skin, delving his tongue into the hollow at the base of her throat. "Who needs coffee and dessert?"

"But..." she began, only to lose her voice in a gasp when he shifted his body lower, causing a delicious friction.

His tongue delved lower, following the neckline of her shirt into the valley of her breasts. She gasped again, shivering when he moved to capture the aching tip of one breast through the silk material of her shirt and bra.

"Ryan...you...we...must stop this," she said, between ragged breaths. "I...I... Oh..." Her voice fled before the onslaught of sensations the suckling pull of his lips sent crashing through her entire being.

Never, never had Lindsay experienced such an intensity of sensual sensations, not even with her husband. It was at once both shaming and exhilarating. For never had she felt more aware of herself as a woman, a mature woman, hungering for the taste, the touch, the possession of a man, the need to possess that man in return.

Ryan shifted positions again, seeking her now open and eager mouth, taking it with a low groan of need.

Where it would have ended...well, Lindsay knew

exactly where it would have ended, had not, at that inopportune moment, a loud and pitiable wailing rent the air, swelling to a screeching, ear-shattering crescendo reverberating throughout the house.

"What in the world?" Ryan exclaimed, jerking back to stare at her with frowning consternation.

Lindsay sighed, but in disappointment or relief, she wasn't sure. "Sheba," she said, giving a gentle push against his chest. "You'd better let me up," she added, raising her voice to be heard over the wailing noise. "She won't quit until I let her out of the bedroom."

Wincing against the racket, cursing under his breath, Ryan levered himself off of her. "Go, quickly," he ordered, raking a hand through his hair. "That racket is enough to set my teeth on edge."

Lindsay was quick to obey, but only because her teeth were already on edge. She dashed for the stairs, stumbling a little when he called after her.

"But keep in mind that that cat hates me, and if that she-devil attacks me again, she's dead."

Convinced by his tones that he would carry through with his threat, Lindsay bolted up the stairs and along the second floor hallway to her room, determined to scoop her pet up into her arms and keep her there until Ryan left—not only for Sheba's protection from him, but her own as well.

She was scolding before she turned the doorknob and swung the door open. "Sheba, stop it at once, before the neighbors start ringing my..." Lindsay broke off, for she was talking to herself; with the quicksilver swiftness of white lightning, Sheba had streaked through the doorway and along the stairs the instant she'd opened the door.

Oh, Lord, she thought, alarmed, tearing after the feline, if Sheba pounced on Ryan... Lindsay came to a halt halfway down the stairs, shaken by the sight that met her surprise-widened eyes. Ryan was sitting bolt upright on the sofa, still and silent, Sheba curled like a scarf around his neck. Since he wasn't cursing, or strangling the animal, she could only hope he was as yet uninjured.

Almost afraid to continue on down the stairs and cross to the sofa for fear of startling Sheba into baring her claws and sinking them into his neck, Lindsay forced herself to move, slowly and carefully.

A soft sigh whispered through her lips as she circled the end of the sofa. Ryan's face was set and rigid, but there were no signs of scratches or blood on his skin or shirt. Quite the opposite, in fact. Though Sheba lay like a boa of white fur around his neck, her eyes were closed and she was nuzzling her little face into the underside of his clenched jaw, purring in blissful contentment.

"Get her off me," Ryan growled through his gritted teeth the moment he spied her.

A wave of mixed relief and amusement rushing through her, Lindsay was hard put to keep a straight face. "It's all right, Ryan, she won't hurt you," she assured him, losing the battle against a smile. "Sheba doesn't hate you at all. Like it or not, I'm afraid you've made a conquest. She obviously loves you. Do you suppose she believes she has found her king?" she mused aloud, giving way to a grin.

"Very funny," he muttered, raising a hand to

reach for the animal paying homage to him with her tiny pink tongue.

"What are you going to do?" she cried, renewed concern for her pet wiping the grin from her face.

Tossing her a wry look, he plucked the cat from his neck, cradled her in his arm, and stroked her with his free hand. "What else?" he finally answered in tones as dry as day old toast. "I'm going to love her back."

Lucky Sheba.

Shocked by the self-revealing thought, Lindsay lifted the still, even louder purring feline from his arm. "I'd better give her supper," she said when he arched that one blasted eyebrow in question. "Before she decides to take a love bite out of you." She turned to head for the kitchen.

In a quick move both liquid and graceful, Ryan stood and placed a staying hand on her arm. "It's getting late, and I'd better get going."

"But you haven't had your coffee and dessert," she said, frowning. "Again."

"No, thanks," he said, drolly and pointedly, "I believe I've had enough stimulation for one evening."

Vividly recalling her part in the most stimulating event of the evening, Lindsay's cheeks grew warm. But he continued before she could respond, or even think of a suitable response.

"I'll take another rain check," he said, a wicked light in his eyes. "Tomorrow evening." Laughing at her startled look, he turned and sauntered to the door.

"But..." Lindsay moved to follow him, but Sheba let out another wail and began wiggling and twisting to get free. It was all Lindsay could do to hold on to the cat, keep her from leaping from her arms to go to Ryan. "What time?" she called, hanging on to Sheba for all she was worth.

"Suppose I stop by after work...say six-thirty or so?" he said, smiling at her efforts to contain the feline.

"Yes, all right. Darn it, Sheba," she cried, becoming frazzled. "Will you settle?"

Laughing, he opened the door. "I'll see you tomorrow. Now, go feed the queen, maybe that will settle her."

Then he was gone, leaving Lindsay breathless, anxious, and wishing the hours away until tomorrow evening.

Chapter Five

Over the course of the remainder of that week, Ryan put forth a concerted effort and a great deal of charm into sweeping Lindsay off her feet. But not in the usual, time-honored tradition often employed by men of wining and dining and romancing women.

Forgoing the advantages of the variety of restaurants, the entertainment venues of theaters, concerts, jazz clubs and other special events available, Ryan concentrated his campaign on the home front... Lindsay's home front.

And he insisted that Lindsay didn't have to lift a finger to help. Although, flustered in a way he found utterly adorable, she in turn insisted on doing so.

Being honest with himself, Ryan conceded to the fact that, in addition to her surface beauty and delicate appearance, he found most things about Lindsay utterly adorable. Everything from her mercurial switches from demure to militantly challenging, to the way her voice softened with love at the mention of her children, to the undeniable attraction that sizzled between them—that she nevertheless tried to deny.

In particular, and by a good measure, Ryan craved the soft, enticing, exciting, honey-sweet taste of Lindsay's adorable mouth.

It was incredible, Ryan reflected throughout the remainder of the week, at odd moments when he was alone. He couldn't remember ever feeling quite the same emptiness of yearning to be with any other woman, not even when he was young and impressionable and in the early days with his former wife.

Ryan was all too aware of how much he wanted to make love with Lindsay, his rioting libido gave ample proof of the force of his desire for her. But, just as compellingly, he simply wanted to be with her, talk with her, laugh with her, and even argue with her. And that kind of wanting he had never in his life experienced before.

Ryan wasn't sure he liked the strange new emotions churning inside him, but he couldn't deny their dictates.

For her part, Lindsay felt caught up in a delightful maelstrom of sensations, brought on by Ryan's single-minded attention to her. Her emotions swirled with dizzying speed from being beguiled by him and exasperated with him.

What worried Lindsay was that she feared beguilement would too quickly hold sway over exasperation. Throughout the rest of the week, she had to work hard at keeping her mind in command of her emotions.

It wasn't an easy task, for Ryan was a formidable mind-altering force.

Each evening he arrived at Lindsay's door laden with seductive offerings consisting of gourmet meals, the finest wines, flowers to grace the table, expensive chocolates to tempt the strongest of wills and always, always a tidbit or toy for the adoring Sheba.

The first evening, over a dinner of succulent shrimp scampi Ryan had specially prepared by the chef of an upscale Philadelphia restaurant, Lindsay had attempted to steer the conversation in the direction of her idea for a wedding reception.

"I had a message on my machine from Ashley when I got home from work today," she said, oh, so casually. "She said they love Italy, their hotel is fabulous, and that they would be returning home a week from next Tuesday."

Fully expecting Ryan to voice some sarcastic remark or opinion, she took a fortifying sip of her wine, then held her breath, eyeing him warily.

"I know," he said, so mildly she nearly went into shock. "I had a similar call from Logan."

Thinking, hoping his strong objections to the couple's elopement had mellowed somewhat, she ventured a gentle probe on the subject. "That's not much time to arrange a reception, even a small one."

Ryan shrugged, and speared a plump shrimp with his fork. "They will already be married three weeks by the time they get home, a few weeks or so longer shouldn't make that much difference," he said, smiling benignly before popping the shrimp into his mouth.

"But…" she began, only to be silenced by an imperious wave of his hand.

"Later," he said.

Later, to Lindsay's inner chagrin, and secret delight, proved much like the night before. She tried to pursue that subject when she joined him in the living room, after starting the coffee, but within minutes, found herself in his arms, drowning in his senses-drenching kisses.

Fortunately, to her relief, and secret frustration, her common sense reasserted itself before she found herself in his arms in her bed.

She eased out of his embrace, and him out the door…again without having his coffee.

The second evening, Ryan showed up at her door bearing a large thermal container, from which he produced a full three-course dinner consisting of chateaubriand and all the trimmings, along with a bottle of a special vintage pinot noir.

Undaunted, Lindsay again broached the forbidden subject during dinner, And once again, Ryan put her off with a negligent wave and a murmured, "Later."

Later turned into a delayed replay of the previous night, with Lindsay lost in his arms, and his mouth. His kisses were increasingly more intense, deeper, hotter. His hands were taking license she had never allowed from another man, testing the limits of her moral fortitude.

By the time she gathered the strength to send him home, yet again without having coffee, she was getting desperate. Never one to lie, especially to herself, Lindsay squarely faced the fact of her nearly overwhelming physical desire for Ryan.

But what was worse, much worse, was the frightening, yet no longer deniable fact that she had fallen in love with him. She had fallen for a man who disdained and strongly objected to the very concept of falling in love so very quickly, if he had ever believed in love at all.

Lindsay spent the majority of that night restless and awake, tormented by her feelings and situation. She longed to be with Ryan, in every definable sense of the word, in and out of the bedroom.

By his actions, Ryan had shown her the man inside, the gentle man he often concealed behind a rough exterior. He baited her, and seemed to enjoy sparking a response from her, but never in a mean or cruel way. But he could be and often was charming, as well. And, since the night Sheba had curled around his neck in feline adoration, he had revealed a tender streak, laughing softly and caressing the cat whenever she coiled around his leg or leaped into his lap, mewing and purring a plea for his attention.

But it had been so long, close to twenty years, since she had been with a man, made love with a man. And to abandon her innate reticence after all this time, merely to abandon herself to a man who gave every indication of being interested in nothing beyond a physical affair...

A few hours before dawn, Lindsay made a decision, firm and irrevocable. She couldn't allow her heart to surrender to the demands of her body. She wanted to, wanted to so badly she actually ached inside. But she couldn't, wouldn't take the risk of suffering a broken heart to appease her body's needs, normal and healthy as they might be.

Whether or not her actions caused friction in their now combined families, and despite the pain she'd be causing herself, Lindsay determined to send Ryan packing, just as soon as she figured out how to go about it.

It was almost funny, Lindsay reflected along around 4:00 a.m. Several years after her husband died, she had turned away from intimacy with the only man she had spent serious time with, simply because she didn't love him. And now, so many years later, she had to turn away from intimacy with another man, simply because she did love him.

Lindsay finally slept, but she wasn't laughing at her almost funny circumstances. She fell asleep with tear streaks drying on her face.

The next evening, Friday, a caterer's van pulled into Lindsay's driveway behind Ryan's car.

"Ryan...what is this?" Lindsay asked at the door, quickly backing as he strode inside.

"Dinner," he said, motioning for the three trailing in his wake to follow him.

In bemusement, Lindsay stood at the dining alcove archway, watching as the one woman and two men proceeded to empty and arrange on the table the contents of the cartons each one had carried into the house.

When they were gone, an array of delicacies covered the table; a variety of salads, finger sandwiches, a basket of assorted rolls, relish and fruit trays, a small crystal bowl of mixed nuts, and another of miniature chocolates, condiments and a bottle of outrageously expensive champagne.

"Well, what do you think?" Ryan arched that one eyebrow over eyes gleaming with a teasing light.

"You're mad," Lindsay declared, having to laugh despite the hollow, unhappy feeling instilled by her nocturnal decision.

"Yeah, maybe," he said, raising a hand to cup her jaw, lift it to his descending mouth. "But it's a sweet madness, and I'm loving every minute of it."

Lindsay gave a brief thought to avoiding his kiss, then thought again. Why deny herself this last evening of delirious pleasure only Ryan could stir within her?

She was breathless, her heart racing, her senses scattered by the time Ryan lifted his mouth from hers. She'd been wrong, she decided. He wasn't mad; she was. Aching for more of the same madness, and yet afraid she'd get lost inside it, she said the first thing that came into her head.

"The...er...food's getting cold."

"It's already cold." A small smile curving his tempting mouth, he drew one finger around her lips, and a shuddering response from her body.

"I'm hungry," she blurted out, desperate to move away from him, desperate to move closer.

His hazel eyes darkened to emerald green. "So am I, so hungry I can hardly stand it."

Oh, Lord. Lindsay's heart thumped, her pulses pounded, her mind headed for stun. Gathering her senses, she caught herself before she could fling herself into his arms. Her movements unsteady, she stepped back, out of harm's way, and turned to the table.

"Then let's eat," she said, too brightly.

Ryan groaned.

Lindsay silently echoed his sound of frustration.

She wasn't hungry, not for food, but to her amazement, after her first bite, her appetite returned. So, apparently, did Ryan's, as between them they wreaked real damage on the selection of delicious foods.

"About the reception," Lindsay hazarded, replete but still nibbling on a tiny orange-filled chocolate.

"Later."

Knowing there would be no later for them, she sighed and got up to start clearing the table. When Ryan rose to help, she insisted he go into the living room and get comfortable, or play with the cat, determined to carry out her middle-of-the-night decision by staying a safe distance from him.

She didn't bother preparing the coffee.

When, after many deep, fortifying breaths, Lindsay entered the living room, Ryan was engaged in a tug-of-war with Sheba over possession of a mangled rag toy.

Poor Sheba, she thought sadly. Her pet would miss Ryan. A tightness gripped Lindsay's throat. A rush of moisture stung her eyes. She had to do it, now, she told herself, before she changed her mind.

Blinking, Lindsay drew another deep breath, planted her hands on her hips, and launched an attack.

"Are you ready now to discuss the wedding reception for Ashley and Logan?"

Without letting go of the rag toy, Ryan angled his head to look at her. "I don't think so," he answered, so damned calmly she wanted to smack him.

"When will you be ready?" she demanded.

He frowned. "What's the hurry?"

"Hurry?" She stared at him in disbelief. "I've been trying to get you to discuss it for most of this past week. I'd hardly call four days a hurry."

"Evenings," he corrected her, grinning.

"Whatever," she retorted, a spurt of anger tempering her feelings of desolation. "But it doesn't matter, does it? You never intended to discuss it, did you?"

"Lindsay," he began, dropping the toy, but, in full spate, she wouldn't let him continue.

"You've been toying with me," she accused, feeling sick and shivery inside, close to tears. "Just like you're toying with Sheba. Only with me, you're playing a much more serious game. Aren't you?"

"Yes," he admitted, getting up to face her.

"All this attention, the dinners, the wine, have been for one purpose. You want to get me into bed. Don't you?"

"Yes...but... Lindsay, listen..."

"No." She wouldn't listen to him, she couldn't; hearing him confirm her suspicions was more than enough. She crossed to the door on shaky legs. "I want you to go."

"Go?" Ryan looked stunned, as if he couldn't believe what she had said. "Lindsay, there's nothing wrong with two people, single and unattached, going to bed together."

There is if only one of those people is in love, she cried in silent anguish. But she couldn't say it to him, couldn't betray herself that way. Bereft of words, she let her actions answer for her. She opened the door.

"Oh, come on, Lindsay," he said, striding to her. "Damn it, you want me as much as I want you." Impatience edged his voice. "Can you deny it?"

"No." Her voice was barely there.

"Then...why are you doing this?" he barked.

"Because I don't play bedroom games." Terrified she'd fall apart if she didn't get him out of there, she stepped back, pulling the door wide after her. "Good night, Ryan."

Ryan spent most of that weekend inside his condo. At intervals, he prowled through the large apartment, cursing a blue streak. His low, harsh voice reverberated inside the rooms, empty of any other living entity.

In between his pacing outbursts, he stood at the huge living room window overlooking Fairmont Park and the Schuylkill River. He stared out, seeing nothing, trying to ignore the tight heaviness in his chest and gut.

He was just tired and overworked, Ryan told himself. Both were true. After two nights of only snatches of sleep, he was tired. And, after the marathon he had performed the previous four days to clear his desk by five-thirty each afternoon, he had overworked himself.

Ryan was also angry. He had every right to be angry, he assured himself, considering the added exertions he had expended after working hours to please one small woman.

All for nothing. Muttering an unprintable expletive, Ryan spun away from the window to resume prowling. Damn it, he stood six foot two in his stocking feet, and that one small woman had booted him out of her house without lifting a hand or one dainty foot.

"Who needs her," he muttered, veering off his now set path into the gleaming, up-to-the-minute kitchen, only to gaze around the room, wondering what in hell he was doing there. He had barely eaten a thing for a day and a half but, though a hunger burned deep inside him, he had no desire for food.

So, okay, his body had needs, Ryan admitted to himself, since denial would have been pointless. So what? He hadn't fixated on Lindsay. Of course not. Hell, there were several women he could think of right off the top of his head who had shown an unabashed eagerness for his company, in public, in private, and in his bed.

Problem was, Ryan knew, inside, where he lived, and dreamed, that he didn't want to be with any one of those other women.

It was midafternoon on Sunday when, standing once more at the window, Ryan heaved a sigh and faced a fact of his suddenly barren life.

He wanted Lindsay.

Squaring his shoulders, Ryan turned and strode with purposeful steps to his bedroom, his bathroom, his shower. Twenty minutes later, he strode from the condo.

Business was brisk at the store on Saturday and Sunday. All the while she dealt with her saleswomen, her customers, an image of Ryan's expression of bafflement and anger as he'd strode from her house, haunted Lindsay.

It was for the best. Lindsay repeated the words to herself like a mantra in hopes of some day believing them. Two nights of precious little sleep were beginning to take their toll, on her nerves and in her appearance. Pale and wan, she looked like hell, and she knew it.

Lindsay just didn't care. That is, until Ryan walked into the store Sunday mere seconds before closing time. She was behind the register, ringing up the sale for the last customer, when she saw him enter, stop to chat with Betty, who had gone to the front to lower the security grate.

Seeing the customer on her way with a plastic smile, Lindsay skirted around the counter to a nearby display table, moving with a nonchalance she was far from feeling. Straightening the merchandise on the table, she surreptitiously monitored his every move.

Ryan said something. Her expression oddly conspiratorial, Betty smiled and nodded. Lindsay felt a pang in her chest when Ryan laughed. The pang intensified, stealing her breath, when he turned and headed directly toward her.

"Okay, I give up," he said when he came to a stop at the other side of the table. "We'll plan your blasted party."

The pang grew worse; did he actually believe the contention between them centered on a wedding reception?

"On one condition." Ryan's tone held a note of finality.

Startled, Lindsay blinked. "Condition?" she repeated. "What condition?"

He hesitated a moment, looking uncertain, almost afraid. Ryan Callahan, uncertain and afraid? The thought zapped through Lindsay's mind as she waited for his response.

"That you marry me," he said, baldly, decisively.

"Marry you?" Lindsay stared at him in stunned disbelief. Was this the man who didn't believe in love at first sight, objected to short acquaintance marriage? But a tiny bud of hope unfurled inside her. She had to ask, "Why?"

"Because I love you, damn it," he confessed, in tones not at all gentle or loving. "So, will you marry me?"

A feeling of joy and serenity settled over Lindsay, revealed in her voice and smile.

"Yes."

Whipping around the table, Ryan pulled her into his arms, crushing her to him as though he'd never let her go. Lowering his head, he captured, for all time, her mouth, and her heart, with his own.

Vaguely, though the mist of love clouding her mind, Lindsay heard Betty and the other two saleswomen cheering.

Three days later, Ryan and Lindsay were ensconced in a suite in one of Atlantic City's finest hotels. Those three days had been a whirl of activity. First thing Monday morning, they had met at a restaurant in Philadelphia to have breakfast together before acquiring a marriage license. Lindsay had spent most of Tuesday tearing around looking for the perfect dress and accessories. Ryan worked until after eight, clearing his desk.

At four that afternoon, at the convenience of a judge who happened to be an acquaintance of Ryan's, they had been married in the judge's chambers.

Through the wide, floor-to-ceiling bedroom window of the suite, the setting sun gilded the undulating waters of the bay and the ocean beyond.

Lying side by side on the king-size bed, replete for the moment, Lindsay and Ryan didn't notice.

The white, almost demur nightgown and negligée Ryan had admired the first day he had entered Lindsay's Intimates, and had instructed Betty to charge to his credit card and have shipped overnight to his office, lay draped over a chair. They didn't notice that, either.

"Tell me you love me." It was a sensuous command from Ryan to his wife.

"I have." Lindsay smiled into his slumberous eyes. "At least a hundred times."

"Tell me again." His voice softened. "Please."

"I love you." Moving with astonishing speed, he rolled over and pinned her beneath him. "I... love...you," he vowed between quick, delicious kisses.

"In that case," Lindsay said, uncertainly, then rushed on, "You won't get mad when I tell you I broke your dictum of silence and called Mary to tell her about us."

That darned eyebrow went up, but his eyes were lit with laughter. "I should punish you," he threatened in a sexy growl. "With kisses."

"Promises, promises," Lindsay taunted, growing breathless with renewed excitement and expectation.

With delightful effect, Ryan proceeded to carry out his threat.

Still later, the glittering lights of the city blazing in the distance through the undraped window, Lindsay lay curled in her husband's arms, content and at peace. Sliding her fingers through the mat of dark curls on his chest, she gazed into his eyes and nibbled on her lip.

"What?" Ryan asked, accurately reading her hesitant expression.

"Darling," she said, coaxingly. "I really think we should let Ashley and Logan know."

"I did."

She frowned. "When? How? Did you call them?"

"No." Pressed to him, she could feel the beginning rumble of laughter deep in his chest. "I faxed them from the office this morning."

"You devil." Lindsay scolded, suppressing a smile.

His laughter escaped, a joyous sound filling the room, blending with her own.

* * * * *

Look for Joan Hohl's next book,
THE DAKOTA MAN, coming in October from
Silhouette Desire.

t, follow directions published in the offer to which you are responding. Contest begins 1/1/00 and ends on 8/24/00 (the "Promotion Period"). Method of entry may vary. Mailed entries must be postmarked by 8/24/00, and received by 8/31/00.

2. During the Promotion Period, the Contest may be presented via the Internet. Entry via the Internet may be restricted to residents of certain geographic areas that are disclosed on the Web site. To enter via the Internet, if you are a resident of a geographic area in which Internet entry is permissible, follow the directions displayed on-line, including typing your essay of 100 words or fewer telling us "Where In The World Your Love Will Come Alive." On-line entries must be received by 11:59 p.m. Eastern Standard time on 8/24/00. Limit one e-mail entry per person, household and e-mail address per day, per presentation. If you are a resident of a geographic area in which entry via the Internet is permissible, you may, in lieu of submitting an entry on-line, enter by mail, by hand-printing your name, address, telephone number and contest number/name on an 8"x 11" plain piece of paper and telling us in 100 words or fewer "Where In The World Your Love Will Come Alive," and mailing via first-class mail to: Silhouette 20ᵗʰ Anniversary Contest, (in the U.S.) P.O. Box 9069, Buffalo, NY 14269-9069; (In Canada) P.O. Box 637, Fort Erie, Ontario, Canada L2A 5X3. Limit one 8"x 11" mailed entry per person, household and e-mail address per day. On-line and/or 8"x 11" mailed entries received from persons residing in geographic areas in which Internet entry is not permissible will be disqualified. No liability is assumed for lost, late, incomplete, inaccurate, nondelivered or misdirected mail, or misdirected e-mail, for technical, hardware or software failures of any kind, lost or unavailable network connection, or failed, incomplete, garbled or delayed computer transmission or any human error which may occur in the receipt or processing of the entries in the contest.

3. Essays will be judged by a panel of members of the Silhouette editorial and marketing staff based on the following criteria:

Sincerity (believability, credibility)—50%

Originality (freshness, creativity)—30%

Aptness (appropriateness to contest ideas)—20%

Purchase or acceptance of a product offer does not improve your chances of winning. In the event of a tie, duplicate prizes will be awarded.

4. All entries become the property of Harlequin Enterprises Ltd., and will not be returned. Winner will be determined no later than 10/31/00 and will be notified by mail. Grand Prize winner will be required to sign and return Affidavit of Eligibility within 15 days of receipt of notification. Noncompliance within the time period may result in disqualification and an alternative winner may be selected. All municipal, provincial, federal, state and local laws and regulations apply. Contest open only to residents of the U.S. and Canada who are 18 years of age or older, and is void wherever prohibited by law. Internet entry is restricted solely to residents of those geographical areas in which Internet entry is permissible. Employees of Torstar Corp., their affiliates, agents and members of their immediate families are not eligible. Taxes on the prizes are the sole responsibility of winners. Entry and acceptance of any prize offered constitutes permission to use winner's name, photograph or other likeness for the purposes of advertising, trade and promotion on behalf of Torstar Corp. without further compensation to the winner, unless prohibited by law. Torstar Corp and D.L. Blair, Inc., their parents, affiliates and subsidiaries, are not responsible for errors in printing or electronic presentation of contest or entries. In the event of printing or other errors which may result in unintended prize values or duplication of prizes, all affected contest materials or entries shall be null and void. If for any reason the Internet portion of the contest is not capable of running as planned, including infection by computer virus, bugs, tampering, unauthorized intervention, fraud, technical failures, or any other causes beyond the control of Torstar Corp. which corrupt or affect the administration, secrecy, fairness, integrity or proper conduct of the contest, Torstar Corp. reserves the right, at its sole discretion, to disqualify any individual who tampers with the entry process and to cancel, terminate, modify or suspend the contest or the Internet portion thereof. In the event of a dispute regarding an on-line entry, the entry will be deemed submitted by the authorized holder of the e-mail account submitted at the time of entry. Authorized account holder is defined as the natural person who is assigned to an e-mail address by an Internet access provider, on-line service provider or other organization that is responsible for arranging email address for the domain associated with the submitted e-mail address.

5. Prizes: Grand Prize—a $10,000 vacation to anywhere in the world. Travelers (at least one must be 18 years of age or older) or parent or guardian if one traveler is a minor, must sign and return a Release of Liability prior to departure. Travel must be completed by December 31, 2001, and is subject to space and accommodations availability. Two hundred (200) Second Prizes—a two-book limited edition autographed collector set from one of the Silhouette Anniversary authors: Nora Roberts, Diana Palmer, Linda Howard or Annette Broadrick (value $10.00 each set). All prizes are valued in U.S. dollars.

6. For a list of winners (available after 10/31/00), send a self-addressed, stamped envelope to: Harlequin Silhouette 20ᵗʰ Anniversary Winners, P.O. Box 4200, Blair, NE 68009-4200.

Contest sponsored by Torstar Corp., P.O. Box 9042, Buffalo, NY 14269-9042.

ENTER FOR
A CHANCE TO WIN*
Silhouette's 20th Anniversary Contest

**Tell Us Where in the World
You Would Like *Your* Love To Come Alive...
And We'll Send the Lucky Winner There!**

Silhouette wants to take you wherever
your happy ending can come true.

Here's how to enter: Tell us, in 100 words or less,
where you want to go to make your love come alive!

In addition to the grand prize, there will be 200
runner-up prizes, collector's-edition book sets
autographed by one of the Silhouette anniversary
authors: **Nora Roberts, Diana Palmer,
Linda Howard** or **Annette Broadrick.**

DON'T MISS YOUR CHANCE TO WIN!
ENTER NOW! No Purchase Necessary

Silhouette®
Where love comes alive™

Visit Silhouette at www.eHarlequin.com to enter, starting this summer.

Name:

Address:

City: State/Province:

Zip/Postal Code:

Mail to Harlequin Books: **In the U.S.:** P.O. Box 9069, Buffalo, NY
14269-9069; **In Canada:** P.O. Box 637, Fort Erie, Ontario, L4A 5X3